gabby wallace skips valentine's day

VALENTINE'S EVER AFTER SERIES

AMBER NICOLE

Gabby Wallace Skips Valentine's Day
Copyright © 2026 Amber Nicole
All rights reserved.

ISBN paperback: 979-8-9897939-7-6

Cover Design by Amber Nicole

For permission requests, contact Amber Nicole at authorambernicole@gmail.com

also by amber nicole

To the One who loved me before I knew how to love myself— Jesus, this is all because of You.

tuesday, february 1st

GABBY

Ashen Mills – 10 miles.

My headlights catch the road sign, reflective letters glowing like they're personally mocking me. I almost laugh. Ten miles from the town I swore I'd never return to.

One year in the city, and what do I have to show for it? A box of office supplies from the marketing firm that laid me off—budget cuts, they said. And friends who are all madly in love, paired off like Noah's ark, planning Valentine's surprises while I pretend to care whether red roses are too cliché.

Gag.

Valentine's Day is in two weeks, and I've made it my mission to skip it entirely. No chocolate, no roses, no pitying looks. Just me, my childhood bedroom, my parents' couch, Netflix, and a gallon of cookie dough ice cream.

The plan? Hide from the world. Maybe cry. Avoid Mom's questions about my "future." Relax before I figure out what comes next—because right now, I have no idea.

I roll the window down despite the February chill, letting night air whip my face. My eyes water —from the cold, obviously. I crank up country music until it fills my sedan. My hand drifts out, fingers cutting through rushing air.

For a second, I'm seventeen again—driving these roads with nowhere to be, pretending the future wasn't terrifying.

My eyes sting harder. Maybe it's the wind. Or maybe it's that the future *is* scary, and I'm driving into it with no GPS and a bank account that's laughing at me.

I crank the radio louder, sing along too off-key to care. At least it drowns out thoughts about failure and being twenty-six with nothing but stolen Post-it notes and bruised pride.

Then something cuts through. A low hum. Mechanical.

Blue and red lights strobe in my rearview mirror.

"Oh, *come on*." I groan, pulling toward the shoulder. "Five minutes from home, and I'm already in trouble."

Not that I'm worried. I know all the cops. Coach

Miller taught me softball. Officer Daniels caught me sneaking into the pool and just said "don't drown." They're practically family.

The lights strobe across my dashboard. Behind me, a figure dismounts a motorcycle.

That is definitely not Coach Miller.

He's tall—really tall—with broad shoulders filling out his uniform. The fabric hugs his chest as he moves.

Then he pulls off his helmet. Dark hair tumbles free, messy from the ride. He shakes his head once and drags a hand through it.

My throat goes completely dry.

This is *not* one of the middle-aged cops from the Fourth of July parade. If law enforcement looked like this in high school, I might've seriously considered a career in petty crime.

I can't stop staring as he strides closer, helmet tucked under one arm, confidence in every step. By the time he reaches my door, I'm leaning closer to the window, needing proof he's real.

Big mistake. My heart thuds. I'm dangerously close to drooling.

Get it together, Wallace.

I roll my window down. "Who are you?"

He leans down. "Excuse me, ma'am?"

Oh no. That voice—rough, low, like gravel wrapped in velvet. And did he just call me *ma'am*?

♡ 3 ♡

I'm twenty-six. That's for church ladies with casse-role dishes.

"Please don't call me ma'am."

His jaw tightens. "License and registration."

So serious. No smile. Just business.

I sigh dramatically, fishing out my wallet. If I get a ticket on top of everything else, it's God confirming my life is a disaster.

I pass him the cards, trying for my sweetest smile. "You're new."

He glances at the license, and his face changes. The stern mask melts into a grin.

"Ahh. Gabriella Wallace. We've been expecting you."

My brows shoot up. "Excuse me?"

"The whole town knows you're coming home for a few weeks," he says, practically beaming. "It's been headline news at the diner for days."

I blink. The whole town? That can't be good. "What's that supposed to mean?" My hands gesture wildly. "Are they taking bets on how fast I'll leave?"

He leans casually against my window. "Just that you're famous around here, Miss Wallace. Welcome-home famous. You've got quite the reputation."

I squint. "Wait... do I know you?" Maybe he's one of those awkward high school boys who finally grew into his legs.

His expression shifts, smile fading to professional coolness. "Do you know why I pulled you over, Miss Wallace?"

I lean back, batting my lashes. "Because you think I'm cute and wanted to ask me on a date?"

For half a second, his lips tilt. Barely there. Then the mask returns. "Seventy in a forty-five. And your tail light's out."

Ouch. Strike one for the Wallace charm.

He starts to turn away, then does a double-take at my license. His expression brightens. "You know... you're not at all what I expected."

I blink. Not what he expected? Too pretty for a ticket? Not tragic enough for gossip?

Either way, this went from bad sitcom to full nightmare.

I groan as he walks back to his bike, thunking my forehead against the steering wheel. The horn beeps sadly. Great. Welcome home, Gabby.

I glance in my rearview. He's straddling his bike, head bent over his notepad. I swear I catch the tiniest smile.

Okay, so he *does* have a personality.

I cross my arms and sink lower. "Figures. The one cop I don't know, and he looks like *that*."

My stomach does a ridiculous flutter—traitor—but I shove it down. Nope. Attraction is not on the menu.

The rumble of boots on pavement gets closer. I

pretend to busy myself straightening receipts. Totally casual.

A sharp rap makes me jump. I roll down the window and he leans in, handing me my license and a slip of paper.

"Slow down," he says simply.

I blink at the ticket. "That's it? You're really giving me a ticket? Not even a chance to plead my case?" I gesture to myself. "Come on—what's not to love?"

His mouth twitches but he doesn't bite. "And fix that taillight."

Before I can fire back, he slides his helmet on and turns away, boots crunching against asphalt. Step by steady step, he walks to his motorcycle.

I look down at the paper, ready to toss it in my purse with my other bad decisions.

But I freeze.

There's another slip tucked underneath.

A phone number. Rough handwriting.

MEET ME AT THE STABLE.
TOMORROW NIGHT – 6PM.

My heart leaps into my throat. Heat floods my cheeks—actual, physical heat. My pulse goes haywire. I squirm like a teenager asked to prom.

This is ridiculous. I don't blush. I don't go on

dates with cops who hand me tickets like party favors.

I glare at the ticket and snort. "Yeah, that's a hard pass. Who asks a girl out *and* fines her?"

I shove both papers in my purse, slam into drive, and stomp the gas. Tires screech, dust flying like some rom-com exit.

That'll show him.

Except... my eyes flick to the rearview mirror.

And I'm smiling. Like a complete idiot.

The smile stretches wider. I can't stop it. My reflection stares back—flushed cheeks, ridiculous grin.

"Stop it," I mutter. "You're not going. You're *not*."

Ten miles until Ashen Mills. Ten miles until I face everything I've been running from.

But for this moment, with wind through my window and that note in my purse, I let myself feel something other than failure.

RHETT

She peels off like she's outrunning herself, tires squealing, dust clouding behind her.

I start my bike and grin. Cute.

Most folks apologize, promise to bake me cookies. Gabby Wallace? She stomps the gas just to prove she's mad. Or pretending to be.

But that smile she was fighting at the end? I caught it. Told me everything I needed to know.

First, it was her mom. Mrs. Wallace, sweet woman with kind eyes and a habit of accidentally running into me at church. "My Gabby's coming home soon, Officer Lawson," she'd say with that hopeful mother's smile. "Smart girl. Real pretty, too. You'll see when she gets here."

By the time Mrs. Clark said, "That girl's gonna shake this town right up," I figured half of Ashen Mills was either rolling out a red carpet or bracing for impact.

Me? I didn't think much of it. People come and go. Gossip swirls in small towns.

But now I get it. One look at Gabriella Wallace behind that wheel—fire in those hazel-brown eyes, sass dripping from every word, sunshine buried under storm cloud energy—and I understand why everyone's buzzing.

She radiates trouble. The good kind. The kind you want to chase.

I've been in Ashen Mills six months. Everyone's friendly. Too friendly. Casseroles at the station, dinner invitations, single women "asking directions."

It's nice. But predictable.

Gabriella? Not predictable.

She looked like she couldn't decide whether to flirt, argue, or roll her eyes. Maybe all three at once. And for the first time since I pinned this badge on, I wanted to laugh right there in uniform.

I didn't, of course. Gotta keep the straight face. But when she asked if I pulled her over because I thought she was cute? If she'd looked a half-second longer, she'd have caught the smile I was fighting.

Holiday spirit. That's what I'll call the note I slipped under her ticket like some teenager passing notes in study hall.

Some people see February and groan. Me? I love Valentine's Day. Always have. After years in Houston seeing the worst of humanity, I need reminders that people still believe in love. Still try for it. Still hope.

The town's quiet as I cruise Main Street. Shop windows dark except the diner still glowing golden. I should head home—got leftovers waiting. But four bare walls and microwaved food don't appeal. Not when I'm wired from thoughts about chestnut-brown hair and that smile she tried to hide.

I park at the Lulu's Cafe. The bell jingles. Coffee and fried chicken hit me immediately.

"Evening, Officer Rhett!" Betty beams from behind the counter. "Trouble tonight?"

I slide onto a stool. "Trouble indeed. Just pulled

the infamous Gabby Wallace over heading into town."

Betty's eyes widen. She gasps. "Well, I'll be. That girl's a handful behind a steering wheel. Remember junior year when she swore that old dirt road was a shortcut?"

From her usual booth, Mrs. Taylor pipes up, wagging her fork. "Remember? She rattled into the parking lot with sparks flying, half the undercarriage dragging. Her poor mama nearly fainted."

Betty chuckles, topping off my coffee. "And senior prank week. She organized it. Talked the whole class into filling Principal Carter's office with balloons. Took him three days to dig his desk out."

I wrap my hands around the warm mug. "Sounds like quite the reputation."

Mrs. Taylor shakes her head, but there's affection. "Wild as a wet hen. Always was. But I'll tell you this, Officer—" She points her fork at me, serious. "She also worked double shifts at the library that summer to help her mama pay the light bill when her daddy got laid off. Folks forget that part."

Betty's voice softens. "Gabby's always had more heart than sense. She'll raise a ruckus, sure. But she's good through and through."

I stir sugar slowly and take a sip. They don't need to convince me. One look tonight and I already knew.

The sass was armor. The grumpiness was protection. But underneath? Someone scared, trying not to show it. Someone hurt, not wanting to risk it again.

I know that look. I've worn it myself.

I nurse the coffee while Betty tends to the other table—an older couple sharing pie, taking turns with the fork. Probably married forty, fifty years. Still here, still choosing each other.

The scene feels easy. Like something I used to imagine but never had. Back in Houston, life was sirens and schedules, cases bleeding together. You ate alone. No one cared if you showed up. The city just kept moving.

Here? People notice. People care.

That's why I volunteered with the church when I moved here. Loading food pantry boxes every Tuesday, helping Mrs. Wallace organize coat drives. Mrs. Wallace is kind. Always smiling, always busy, always taking care of everyone else first.

Now I know where Gabby gets it. That fierce independence. That tendency to give more than she takes. That stubbornness wrapped in generosity.

By the time I drain the mug and leave a ten for a five-dollar coffee, the town's mostly asleep. Pharmacy closed, bookstore dark, gas station on emergency lighting.

My apartment's above the hardware store,

accessed by a creaky external staircase. The wood needs replacing, but Mr. Kinley keeps saying "next month" and I keep saying I don't mind. Truth is, I kind of like the sound. Reminds me someone's home.

I climb slowly, boots heavy on each step, and unlock the door—one lock, not three like Houston.

It's simple. Bed against the far wall, couch facing a TV I barely turn on, kitchen table with two chairs even though I eat alone. But it's mine. Four walls and a roof where I can finally breathe.

I toss my helmet on the counter, kick off my boots, and stretch out on the bed without changing. The ceiling fan hums overhead.

I should get up. Brush my teeth. Change. Do the responsible thing.

But I don't move.

My mind's anything but quiet.

I keep replaying it. Her face when she realized I was actually giving her a ticket. The sass when she asked if I pulled her over for a date. The way she tried not to smile at the note. The dramatic stomp on the gas like she had something to prove.

She's back for a reason. Job gone, future uncertain, probably feeling like she failed even though coming home isn't failure. It's just life. Messy and complicated.

I get it. I came here six months ago for my own reasons. Burnout that felt like drowning. A shooting that went wrong—not my fault, the investigation cleared me, but that doesn't stop the 3 AM replays. A city that stopped feeling like opportunity and started feeling like a cage.

I flip onto my side, grinning in the dark. Like a teenager with a crush. Like someone who hasn't felt this anticipation in years—the good kind, the hopeful kind.

She probably tossed that slip straight in her purse. Probably muttered something sarcastic about cops with too much confidence. Probably told herself she's definitely not meeting me tomorrow night.

But tomorrow? Six o'clock at The Stable?

I have a feeling she'll be there.

And if not, I'll see her around town. This is Ashen Mills. Population 3,847. You can't hide here.

I've got time. Patience is one thing the city never took from me.

Lord, theres this girl...Gabby.

I stare at the ceiling fan.

She came flying back into town, literally, and I don't know why but I feel a pull to her.

The fan keeps spinning.

I don't know if You want me to be her friend, but I'm willing.

A pause.

And Lord, if I'm being honest—I like her. Even though I just met her.

I take a breath.

In Jesus' name, amen.

Whatever happens with Gabby Wallace, I know one thing: this isn't a coincidence.

God's up to something.

And I'm curious to see what it is.

wednesday, february 2nd

GABBY

I was supposed to be in Dallas, killing it at my dream job, climbing the ladder.

Then one random Tuesday in January, I walked in to find my boss waiting. That look—your life's about to change, not in a good way.

"Restructuring." "Downsizing." "Budget cuts." "Nothing personal."

Cool corporate words for "we don't need you, pack your desk by noon."

My lease was up anyway. My savings account was laughable—more of a suggestions account. Couch-surfing felt like the next logical step.

Then I blinked, packed what fit, left the rest at Goodwill, and drove home with my tail between my legs.

Now here I am—twenty-six, unemployed, back in my hometown, hiding from Valentine's Day and all things that have to do with love like it's a warrant for my arrest.

My mom and I are at the grocery. I'm navigating through people debating dinner options while Mom stops every three feet.

The freezer section is blessed relief. I scan shelves with focus. There—the last tub of chocolate chip cookie dough. I snatch it, cradling it like gold, then grab backup: double fudge brownie. Maybe a third. Just in case.

Mom wheels up, humming. "Oh, that reminds me," she says casually. Too casually. "I could use your help with Hearts and Hands tomorrow afternoon."

I freeze mid-reach. "The what now?"

"The Valentine's event the church puts on at Ashen Mills Assisted Living. Remember?"

Oh, I remember. Folding tables, red tablecloths, Valentine Bingo, Mrs. Henderson always winning.

"No, Mom." I plop ice cream into the cart. "I'm here to *skip* anything Valentine's related. That's my whole plan. Zero romance."

Mom sighs—the guilt-inducing sigh perfected over decades. "Gabriella, this isn't about you."

Ouch. Direct hit.

"Those residents don't get many visitors," she

continues softly. "Some don't have family at all. They look forward to this every year."

I study the freezer shelves, avoiding her eyes.

"I've already lost four volunteers. The Hendersons are in Florida, Clara's got the flu, the Millers backed out for their grandbaby's recital. I just need you for this one thing."

I glance over. Her face is soft, hopeful, with just enough sparkle to make me cave.

"What kind of 'one thing'?"

"Nothing big," she promises. "Just sorting storage. Two hours, tops."

"Just sorting? No actual event involvement?"

"Just sorting."

"*Fine.*" I grab another carton—cookies and cream. "But that's it."

Mom smiles like she won the lottery. "Of course, honey."

~

I sit cross-legged on my childhood bed, the same faded purple quilt from ninth grade stretched beneath me, staring at the slip of paper in my hand.

Rhett Lawson's handwriting, bold and confident.

MEET ME AT THE STABLE.

TOMORROW NIGHT — 6PM.

I flip it over, then back. Like maybe the reverse side will reveal a hidden message: *Just kidding, don't take me seriously.*

But no. Still there. Still grinning at me in ink.

Yesterday's a blur. Coming home to my parents waiting on the porch. Dinner around the table, Dad's familiar prayer, Mom passing rolls. Comfortable in a way that makes me forget I'm supposed to be figuring out my life.

I flop backward, springs squeaking. Dinner with Rhett.

Pros: He's objectively attractive. Criminally so. The uniform, the voice, everything I shouldn't be noticing.

Cons: This is Ashen Mills. If I show up at The Stable with Rhett Lawson, it won't just be dinner—it'll be headline news. The whole town will decide it's a date.

Besides, I didn't come back here to flirt with anyone. I came to skip Valentine's Day. Hide. Eat ice cream. Figure out what's next.

So no. This cannot be a date.

My phone buzzes. Lila posted a photo—clutching a giant teddy bear. *Day Two of Valentine's countdown! Yesterday flowers, today this guy. What a man.*

My nose wrinkles. "Ew. So gross."

Who needs a stuffed animal that big? It's not cute, it's a storage problem.

I stare at the invitation again. Maybe I don't have to make this romantic. Maybe I can turn it into a bet. If I win, he pays my ticket. That's $175 I desperately need. If he wins...I'll figure that out later. Something humiliating but harmless.

I told myself I wasn't going. Then I remember that smile and apparently lose all reason because suddenly my bed looks like a clothing explosion. Dresses, tops, half my suitcase dumped everywhere.

Finally, I settle on faded jeans and a slouchy brown sweater that slips off one shoulder. Effortless, not "I tried for an hour." Even though I actually did.

Hair down in loose waves. Tan flats.

I study my reflection. One eyebrow arches back skeptically.

"Relax," I mutter. "This isn't a date. It's strategy."

I slip Rhett's note into my pocket. "I know exactly what my bet's going to be."

RHETT

The Stable is buzzing tonight—families still here before the eight o'clock grown-up crowd takes over. Neon lights hum, country band tuning up, kids in cowboy hats racing past.

From my table near the dance floor, I've got a view of everything. Pool tables, darts, and that mechanical bull in the corner. I shake my head looking at it. Heck to the no.

The waitress pauses. "You sure you don't want to order, sugar?"

I glance at my watch. 6:45. She's late. Assuming she even shows.

"Not yet. Just a few more minutes."

She nods sympathetically. She's probably seen this exact scenario a hundred times—guys waiting for dates that never show.

I lean back, trying to look casual, but my eyes keep darting to the door. Any second now, I tell myself.

Or never. Which seems just as likely.

I rub my neck, about to signal the waitress after all, when the door swings open.

And there she is.

For a second, the noise fades. Just her, framed in the doorway.

She came. She actually came.

I stand as she weaves through the crowd. When she reaches me, I pull out her chair.

She quirks an eyebrow. "This isn't a date, Officer Lawson."

I grin. "Of course not, Miss Wallace. Just two new friends, sharing a meal at the most romantic spot in town."

Her laugh is short and skeptical. "Romantic? Please. This place smells like beer and bad decisions."

"Some of the best nights smell like beer and bad decisions," I say.

The waitress drops menus and disappears.

Gabby crosses her arms, leaning back. Challenge in her eyes.

"C'mon, Gabriella," I say, leaning forward.

She stops me cold with a glare. "Don't call me that. It's Gabby."

"Gabby," I let the name roll off slow. "If this isn't a date... then what is it?"

Without breaking eye contact, she reaches into her purse. The ticket I gave her lands on the table with a sharp little plop.

"If I win," she says, "you pay my ticket."

"Win at what?"

Her gaze flicks across the room. Lands on the corner.

The mechanical bull.

Oh no. Oh *heck* no.

Her lips curl into the smuggest grin. "Whoever can stay on the longest wins."

I huff out a laugh, shaking my head. "So let me get this straight. If you win, I pay for the ticket you earned going twenty-five over." I pause. "And if I win..."

She leans forward, anticipating.

"You dance with me. Right there." I nod toward the dance floor. "Three songs."

Her chair scrapes back. "Absolutely not."

"Why?" I sit back, smirking. "Afraid you're gonna lose?"

Her eyes flash. In an instant she's on her feet, chin high. "Bring it on, tough guy."

Before I can blink, she's striding toward the bull. Every head in the room turns.

The waitress reappears. "So, you two ready to order?"

I stand, grinning. "We'll be back in a bit."

I trail after her. "Ladies first," I call, sweeping my hand toward the bull.

Gabby flashes me a mischievous grin and swings onto the bull with surprising ease.

"Max speed," she tells the operator.

He pauses, toothpick dangling. "Uh, you sure 'bout that, miss?"

"Yep." She points at me. "And for him too."

The operator chuckles. "Don't say I didn't

warn ya."

Gabby adjusts her grip, nods once, and the bull jerks to life.

My jaw nearly hits the floor.

She doesn't flinch. Doesn't squeal. Instead, she *moves* with it—hips swaying, hair flying. The neon lights flicker over her, casting her in flashes of wild energy.

The bull bucks hard, twisting, finally sending her tumbling into the padded side. She lands with a laugh, popping right back up.

She steps out, brushing hair from her face, and tosses me a wink. "Your turn, Lawson. Six seconds. Gotta beat that. Which you won't."

I bark out a laugh. "You're enjoying this way too much."

"You bet I am."

I take a breath and swing onto the bull, trying to look smooth even as my pulse hammers.

The operator smirks. "Max speed, right?"

I shoot Gabby a look. She just smiles sweetly.

"Bring it on," I mutter, gripping the rope.

The bull bucks once. Twice. I tighten my grip, jaw locked. Three. Four. Five. Six seconds hit, and I'm still hanging on when it finally kicks me loose.

The crowd erupts—cheers, applause, whistles.

I spot Gabby leaning against the gate, mouth hanging open.

"Six and a half," I say, brushing dust from my jeans. "Guess that makes me the winner."

Her eyes narrow, but there's a spark there.

"Time to pay up, Miss Wallace." I offer my hand.

After a long beat, she slides hers into mine. Her palm is warm, smaller than mine.

"Three dances," I remind her, voice low. "That was the deal."

Before she can argue, the sharp chirp of my phone cuts through the music.

Dispatch. *All units requested. Possible brawl at the bowling alley.*

I exhale, half groan, half laugh. "Of course."

"What is it?"

"Bowling alley chaos. League night. Someone always accuses someone of cheating. Couple punches, a flying shoe or two—it's tradition."

She shakes her head, laughing. "That's your big emergency?"

"Hey, never underestimate a man armed with a bowling ball and wounded pride." I drop cash on our table to cover drinks. Then I meet her eyes.

"I'll be seeing you, Gabby Wallace." I take a step back, grin tugging at my mouth. "And don't think for a second I've forgotten—you still owe me three dances."

Her lips part, just slightly, cheeks flushing.

And then I'm gone.

I'm halfway down the block when I glance back through the window.

She's still standing there. Still watching me leave.

Still smiling too.

thursday, february 3rd

GABBY

I steer my car toward the church, already bracing for whatever mountain of dusty boxes Mom has waiting. Not exactly how I wanted to spend Thursday—which I wanted to spend in bed scrolling through job postings I'm not qualified for and eating cereal straight from the box.

Last night still plays in flashes. The mechanical bull. My confident six seconds. His smug six and a half. That grin when he slid off like he'd been born on that thing. Then his hand offered for a dance, my heart doing actual gymnastics, before dispatch chirped and reality crashed back in.

Thank God for that call. It saved me from three dances with a man who smells like leather and confidence and makes my brain go fuzzy.

I've got enough to handle without a hot cop making me wonder things. Things like what his hands would feel like on my waist. Whether he's this charming with everyone.

Nope. Not going there.

Still, I can't deny it: he checks almost every box. Kind. Check. Funny. Check. Good with families. Check. Employed with a stable job. Check. Looks incredible in uniform. Double check with gold stars.

Which is exactly why I need to keep my head down and stay far away.

The second I step through the church doors, I'm swallowed by chaos. Bins stacked high, boxes spilling red and pink decorations like Valentine's Day threw up in here, pop-up tables covered in tangled streamers. Volunteers buzz around like disorganized bees.

Someone's arguing about tablecloth colors. Mrs. Henderson's trying to untangle a massive ball of ribbon that looks like it survived a war.

Mom's in the middle, papers clutched like battle plans, phone wedged against her ear. Her hair's escaping its normally perfect bun—always a sure sign she's three minutes from unraveling.

"Mom." I wave, dodging a volunteer carrying a life-sized cardboard Cupid.

She spins, relief flooding her face. "Oh, thank goodness. Station two—over there." She points vaguely without looking. "Just start sorting."

I sigh and start weaving between boxes. I'm dodging volunteers, trying not to trip, when I finally look up at station two.

I freeze mid-step.

Of course. Of *course*.

Rhett Lawson stands there in jeans and a simple gray henley that should be illegal, sleeves pushed up to his elbows, sorting through decorations with intense focus. When he sees me, his whole face lights up.

That grin. That stupid, perfect grin that makes my stomach do things stomachs should not do.

"Well, well. If it isn't the famous Gabby Wallace." His voice is warm, teasing.

I arch a brow, falling back on sarcasm like a shield. "Don't believe everything you hear."

He chuckles. "Maybe not everything—but I'm willing to find out which parts are true."

I grab supplies from the bin—scissors, tape, a roll of tangled red ribbon—more to keep my hands busy than because I know what I'm doing. "Glad to know my reputation's alive and well. Small towns really know how to keep legends alive."

He studies me, head tilted, that easy grin softening. "You okay? You seem off. Not the same woman who challenged me to a bull ride last night."

I let out a breath somewhere between a laugh and a groan. "I'm fine. Just didn't really want to help with this Valentine's thing. Shocking, given my deep and abiding love for the holiday."

"Ah, the season of love." His eyes actually brighten like Valentine's Day brings him personal joy. "My favorite time of year."

"Of course it is." I can't help the smirk. "Let me guess—you go all out? Roses, chocolates, probably serenade old ladies at the diner while they eat pancakes?"

He leans against the table, unbothered. "Guilty as charged. Every holiday deserves a little magic. Valentine's Day happens to be top of the list. What's not to love? Love itself, chocolate, an excuse to make people feel special?"

I shake my head, genuinely baffled. "I'm in town for one reason—to skip Valentine's Day entirely. No hearts, no flowers, no chocolate, no pressure. Just me, my parents' couch, and enough ice cream to make a cardiologist weep."

His brows lift. "Skip it? That's practically a crime around here. I might have to write you a citation."

"Then call the cops," I shoot back without missing a beat. "Oh wait—you *are* the cops."

He grins wider, that teasing glint back. "You really don't like Valentine's Day?"

"About as much as I like traffic tickets," I say dryly. "Or root canals. Or those automated customer service loops."

He laughs—really laughs, head thrown back. "You are something else, you know that?"

"And you," I say, crossing my arms, "are a walking Hallmark movie. I'm half expecting you to spontaneously rescue a puppy."

He doesn't even deny it. "Someone's got to balance out all your grumpiness."

I roll my eyes but I'm fighting a smile. I grab balloons from the box. "I know you aren't from here. What brought you to Ashen Mills anyway? You seem too polished for small-town life. Shouldn't you be chasing carjackers or starring in crime shows?"

He quirks a brow. "Polished? Thought you'd go with 'uptight' or 'rule-obsessed.'"

"Don't tempt me." I grin despite myself. "Seriously though, why here? The worst you'll get is rednecks setting off fireworks in bathtubs or Granny Tilda's goat breaking into Dollar General. Last month, the goat ate $47 worth of beef jerky."

That earns a genuine laugh. He sets his clipboard down, leaning against the table, and something shifts—less cop, more just person. "You're not wrong. But Houston..." His smile fades. "Houston drained me. Eight years on the force there, I saw just about every terrible thing a person can do. Violence, cruelty, things I can't unsee. It eats at you, gets into your bones."

I watch his jaw tighten, eyes going somewhere darker.

He shrugs, the moment passing. "A buddy mentioned Ashen Mills was hiring. I sent in an application half-thinking nothing would come of it, got the call two weeks later. Best decision I ever made. Small-town calls, friendly people, actual community. I love knowing people's names, actually helping instead of just responding to emergencies. The worst thing most days is Mrs. Patterson's cat stuck in a tree."

There's relief in his voice. Peace. Gratitude. It makes me forget, for half a second, that I swore off men for the entire month of February.

We fall into easy rhythm after that, sorting decorations, arguing about whether glitter is necessary evil or just evil, laughing at hideous cupid figurines someone donated. By the time we finish, there's more laughter than work, and I've forgotten my defensive walls.

I'm doubled over, clutching my side because Rhett just told me about someone calling 911 because their neighbor's garden gnome was giving threatening looks, when Mom suddenly appears beside us.

"Aw," she coos, eyes lighting up, "I'm so glad you two have finally met. You seem to really get along."

I straighten, catching my breath. "Met? Mom, remember two days ago when I came home crying about the ticket?"

Mom waves dismissively. "Water under the bridge. You two look so happy together."

Rhett's fighting a grin.

"Would you like to join us for dinner tonight?" Mom asks him. "Frank would love to meet you properly."

My eyes widen. "Mom—"

"I'd love to," Rhett says, looking directly at me.

Great. Just great.

"Six o'clock sharp," Mom says, already walking away. "Don't be late!"

I turn to Rhett. "You don't have to—"

"I want to." His smile is genuine. "If that's okay with you."

I sigh, but I'm smiling despite myself. "Fine. But fair warning—my dad's going to interrogate you."

"I can handle it."

RHETT

Standing on the Wallace front porch at 6 PM sharp, I've got a bouquet of daisies in one hand and a bottle of wine in the other, second-guessing everything.

The door swings open before I can knock.

Frank Wallace—broad-shouldered, graying hair, wearing suspenders that somehow look both practical and intimidating. He extends a hand. "Rhett Lawson. Heard a lot about you."

His grip is firm. Testing.

"All good things, I hope, sir."

"Depends on who you ask." His eyes twinkle, but there's definitely an assessment happening.

Christie appears, practically bouncing. "Rhett! Come in, come in!" She spots the flowers. "Oh, how sweet!"

I hand them over. "For you, ma'am."

"You're precious." She accepts them, then eyes the wine. "That's thoughtful, but we don't drink in this house. Personal choice, nothing against those who do."

My face heats. "I'm sorry, I should've asked—"

"No harm done." She pats my arm. "We'll save it for cooking. Wine makes a lovely sauce."

Gabby emerges from the kitchen, hair pulled back in a ponytail, wearing an oversized sweater that somehow makes her look younger. She stops when she sees me.

"Hey," I say, suddenly feeling like I'm sixteen again.

"Hey." Her cheeks flush slightly.

Dinner smells incredible—pot roast, mashed

potatoes, green beans, homemade rolls. The table's set with actual cloth napkins. This is the real deal.

We settle around the table, Frank at the head, and he bows his head without preamble. "Lord, thank You for this food and the company around this table. Bless this meal and guide our conversation. In Jesus' name, amen."

"Amen," I echo.

Christie starts passing dishes immediately. "So Rhett, how are you liking Ashen Mills so far?"

"Love it, ma'am. After Houston, this feels like coming home. The pace is different, but in a good way."

Frank nods, cutting into his pot roast. "Christie mentioned you were big city before this. What made you leave?"

I set down my fork, choosing honesty. "Burnout, mostly. Eight years seeing the worst of people takes a toll. The city's great for some folks, but I needed somewhere I could breathe again. Help people instead of just responding to emergencies. Make a difference in smaller ways."

"That takes courage," Frank says, meeting my eyes. "Admitting when you need a change. Most folks stay stuck in situations that drain them because they're afraid of what leaving means."

Gabby's watching me, something soft in her expression.

"Are you settling in well?" Christie asks. "Finding everything you need?"

"Yes, ma'am. Everyone's been welcoming. Almost too welcoming—I've got more casseroles in my fridge than I know what to do with."

Frank chuckles. "That's Ashen Mills for you. Feed first, ask questions later."

"And you volunteer at church!" Christie beams. "That's wonderful."

"Trying to stay involved. Community's important, and it's what my dad always did. He believed serving others was how you serve God."

After dinner, Gabby and I tackle the dishes without being asked. She washes, I dry.

"Your parents are great," I say, accepting a plate from her.

"They like you." She hands me another. "Which is dangerous."

"Dangerous how?"

"They'll start planning things. More dinners. Holidays. Probably our wedding by next week."

I laugh. "Bit premature, don't you think?"

She flicks soap suds at me. They land on my shirt.

"Oh, it's like that?" I scoop suds from the sink, dotting her nose with bubbles.

Her jaw drops. "You did not just—"

"I absolutely did."

She retaliates, aiming for my face. I dodge. She gets my shoulder instead.

We're laughing, both covered in bubbles, when Christie walks in.

"Well." She crosses her arms, fighting a smile. "I see you two are getting along just fine."

Gabby's face goes crimson. "Mom, we're just—"

"Just cleaning up!" I say quickly.

Christie shakes her head, grinning. "Uh-huh. Gabby, don't forget—supply run tomorrow afternoon for the event. Two o'clock."

"Wait, what—"

"Night, Rhett! So glad you could join us!" Christie disappears back down the hall.

Gabby groans. "I am so sorry. She's relentless."

"Don't be." I dry my hands on the towel. "I had a great time. Your family's wonderful."

At the door, she walks me out onto the porch. The night air is cool, crickets chirping in the background. The porch light casts soft glow over everything.

"Thanks for coming," she says. "Even with my mom ambushing you and my dad interrogating you."

"Wouldn't have missed it." I mean it, too.

She looks up at me, and for a moment it's just us. The night. The quiet.

"See you tomorrow?" I ask. "For the supply run?"

She sighs, but she's smiling. "Apparently so. Mom's already decided."

"Looking forward to it."

I head to my truck, grinning the whole way. Behind me, I hear the door close softly, and I could swear I catch Gabby watching me from the window.

Yeah. This was a good night.

friday, february 4th

GABBY

"This is the last thing I'm helping with," I announce, snapping my seatbelt.

Rhett glances at me, turning the key. His truck roars to life—leather, coffee, and something woodsy. "Heard you the first three times."

"Just making sure we're clear."

"Crystal."

Dollar General's yellow sign buzzes overhead. I slide out, arms crossed. "I'll grab the cart."

"Nope." He steers one free, wheel squealing. "Town safety includes keeping you from mowing down civilians."

"I've never run over anyone with a cart."

"Yet." He winks.

I trail after him, muttering, "This is going to be a nightmare."

The Valentine's aisle looks like Cupid exploded. Pink and red everywhere. Hearts on hearts. Teddy bears. Fake roses. Towers of conversation hearts.

"This is too much," I say.

"This is not nearly enough," Rhett says simultaneously, grabbing heart-shaped balloons.

I swing around. "Are you serious? This is tacky on steroids. Who needs fourteen shades of pink?"

"People who want to smile." He holds up a massive balloon bag. "We'll need at least a hundred."

"A hundred? That's a fire hazard. Fifty, maximum."

"You're heartless."

"I'm practical." I yank the bag back. "If you try inflating all those, you'll pass out and it'll be my fault."

"So you'll help me?" His grin widens, dimples appearing.

"That's not what I said."

"You implied it."

"Did not."

We're glaring at each other when a little boy walks by and asks his mom, "Why do married people always fight?"

My face flames. "We're not married."

Rhett coughs into his fist, shoulders shaking.

I stomp toward the candy aisle. Conversation hearts mock me. "UR CUTE." I read as I grab a box off the shelf. "How riveting."

Rhett plucks it from my hand. "It's a classic."

"It's embarrassing."

"You never got these growing up?"

"Maybe in second grade. Back when you had to hand valentines to every kid or risk social annihilation."

"Ah, the golden years." He drops three packs in the cart.

"Who said we're buying those?"

"Officer's orders."

I swear, if looks could kill, he'd be face-down in a pile of glitter hearts right now.

I toss a package of red streamers into the cart, only buying things from our list, and Rhett immediately reaches for a stuffed bear the size of a toddler.

"You are not putting that in," I say.

"Why not?" He tucks it under his arm like a sidekick.

"Because this isn't Build-A-Bear. We're decorating a nursing home, not traumatizing the residents with giant plush rodents."

"Rodents?" He raises a brow. "You just called a teddy bear a rodent."

"If the shoe fits." I shove it back on the shelf. The

bear stares at me with glassy eyes, and I swear it looks offended.

He chuckles. "You always this heartless, or is it just stuffed animals you've got it out for?"

"Just the fluffy ones that symbolize emotional manipulation."

"That's...oddly specific." He leans his forearms on the cart, studying me with that half-smile that should be illegal. "So, Gabby Wallace, Ashen Mills' very own Grinch—what was it like growing up here? Always hated Valentine's Day, or is that a recent development?"

I shrug, pretending to scan a shelf of chocolates. "The hating Valentine's thing came later. Growing up here was fine. Everyone knew everyone's business, same as now. You sneeze, and by lunch break the town newsletter's got a headline about it."

"Sounds about right," he says, his grin widening. "You one of those kids who couldn't wait to get out?"

"Pretty much. I left after high school and swore I'd never come back."

"And yet," he says, gesturing to the overflowing cart, "here you are—buying pink heart-shaped nonsense with a cop you just met."

I point at him. "Correction, I'm supervising. You're the one who thinks we need confetti cannons."

"Confetti makes everything better."

I roll my eyes, but I'm smiling. I find the last item —heart-shaped cookie cutters—and check it off our list.

Somewhere between aisle seven and Rhett convincing me love-themed napkins were essential, I stopped counting how many times he made me laugh.

He's chatting with the cashier now, that easy grin making her blush. Meanwhile, I'm pretending not to notice how his sleeves stretch over his forearms.

Stop. Noticing. Things.

The conveyor groans under balloon weight, candy, streamers, and items I don't remember agreeing to.

"This is officially the last thing," I declare. "Don't ask me again."

"I know, you've said it twenty times in the last hour." He doesn't even look up, just swipes his card and nods politely at the cashier.

The truck smells the same on the way home— leather, coffee, woodsy cologne. The heater hums. I press my forehead to the cold glass, watching bare trees flick past in a blur.

I feel him glance at me, but I don't turn my head. If I do, I might catch him smirking again, and I don't need that burned into my brain.

When he turns, I expect to see my parents'

driveway. Instead, the truck rumbles past it and heads toward the church parking lot.

"Wait," I say, sitting up straighter. "Why are we here?"

He taps the steering wheel. "We have to drop supplies off. You didn't think we'd leave this in my truck?"

I guess that's fair.

He parks, throws the truck in park, and hops out before I can argue. I drag my feet after him, arms full of bright yellow bags. The side doors of the fellowship hall are propped open, and inside I can hear the hum of volunteers sorting and stacking.

Perfect. More witnesses to my slow descent into community service.

Together we haul the bags inside, the cart squeaking like it's protesting just as much as I am. The room smells faintly of lemon cleaner and old wood, and pop-up tables are lined with bins labeled in my mom's handwriting:

Decorations

Ballons

Candy

Misc.

Rhett starts unloading with military precision, dropping everything exactly where it belongs. I, on the other hand, toss a bag of glitter hearts onto the "MISC." table and dust my hands off like my work here is done.

"Real helpful," he teases, sliding the candy neatly into place.

"Don't push it, Lawson. I said this was the last thing, and I meant it."

He doesn't say a word—just smirks and keeps stacking.

I roll my eyes and turn toward the door, muttering under my breath. Last thing. Definitely the last thing.

RHETT

I finish sorting the last of the streamers and glance up again, just to watch her tuck a strand of hair behind her ear while she listens intently to Mrs. Johnson, one of the oldest ladies in Ashen Mills.

I walk up to Gabby just in time to hear Mrs. Johnson say, "I am just so happy to see you and Officer Lawson together—you two are going to make the cutest babies."

Gabby's face goes crimson. Her mouth opens, then closes, then opens again, like she's buffering.

I should probably save her from her mortification.

But where's the fun in that?

I plaster on my most charming grin and step right up beside her. "Hey, sweetheart, you ready?"

The look she gives me could set off a speed trap. Death by glare. But underneath it, I catch the tiniest flicker of gratitude—mixed with pure, murderous intent.

"Yes, sweetheart," she says, dragging out the word like it personally offends her tongue. "Sorry, Mrs. Johnson, we've got to go!"

Then she hooks her arm through mine. I'm pretty sure it's mostly so she can dig her nails into my sleeve, but still.

Mrs. Johnson clasps her hands like she's watching the opening scene of a Hallmark movie. "Oh, you two just look darling together!"

"Don't encourage him," Gabby mutters through her teeth, smiling tight for the old lady's benefit as she yanks me toward the doors.

Once we're outside, she finally lets go and spins on me. "Sweetheart? Really?"

I shrug, trying not to laugh. "What? I was improvising. You looked like you were about to fake your own death."

"Next time," she says, pointing at me, "let me die."

"Can't do that," I say easily, opening the truck door for her. "Public safety's my job."

She groans, climbing in. "You're impossible."

"Maybe," I say, circling around to the driver's side, still grinning. "But admit it, I make a pretty good fake boyfriend."

Her silence lasts exactly three seconds before she mutters, "You're lucky Mrs. Johnson was watching, or I'd have hit you with a balloon pump."

I chuckle as I start the engine. "Worth it."

~

The drive back to Gabby's is quiet. She doesn't look at me, just keeps her face turned toward the glass, heater fogging the window. She traces a circle in condensation without realizing.

I steal a glance. She looks stubborn, sharp edges everywhere. But the truth is, she shows up. Even when she swears it's the last time.

That's the thing about Gabby Wallace—she talks tough, but her heart keeps betraying her.

I park in her driveway, engine rumbling. She unbuckles fast, grabs bags, mutters "See you later," then disappears inside.

I sit there, staring at the closed door, fighting the grin tugging at my mouth.

She thinks this is her last thing. That she can keep distance.

But something tells me Gabby Wallace isn't done yet.

~

I let the truck idle down Main Street, bleeding off the grin. Lulu's Cafe glows. I pull in, figuring coffee will keep my hands busy while my brain stops replaying Gabby's laugh.

The bell chirps. Betty lifts her chin, already reaching for a cup. "Afternoon, Officer. Sit or sip?"

"Sit." I slide onto a barstool.

From the corner booth, I hear the whisper-hiss of church ladies.

"...I heard Christie set this whole thing up to get her daughter to meet a nice man," someone whispers.

I don't move. The trick with small-town gossip is sitting very still.

"He's polite," Mrs. Dunlap says.

"Tall," Mrs. Hargrove adds reverently. "You can reach the good mixing bowls with a tall one."

"And those shoulders." Mrs. Pruitt. "He could carry the Thanksgiving turkey without breathing hard."

"Does he iron his shirts?" Mrs. Dunlap again. "A man who irons is a man who plans."

Betty slides me coffee and a cookie, hiding her smile.

"I saw him at Dollar General," Mrs. Dunlap continues. "Arguing about balloons with Gabby like they were negotiating the Treaty of Versailles."

"Arguing?" Mrs. Pruitt gasps, delighted. "Oh, they'll be married by fall."

"Question is," Mrs. Hargrove lowers her voice, "does he love the Lord?"

"Oh, he sits third row every Sunday," Mrs. Dunlap answers triumphantly. "My Harvey said the boy even said amen out loud."

Collective approval murmur.

"Christie's clever," Mrs. Hargrove continues. "Get that girl volunteering where the good men are."

"Does he have a boat?" Mrs. Hargrove wonders. "Boats are good for families."

"Cooler's more useful," Mrs. Pruitt decides. "Boats drown marriages. Coolers unite picnics."

I bite my cheek. *Coolers unite picnics* is going on a t-shirt.

"And he helped Christie clean up after the chili cook-off last month," Mrs. Dunlap adds. "Stayed and stacked chairs without being asked. A chair-stacking man is husband material."

"Amen!" Mrs. Hargrove praises.

"Anyway," Mrs. Pruitt finishes, "the Lord works in mysterious ways. Sometimes His ways look like helium and streamers."

Betty snorts. I tip her extra just for surviving this.

I finish my coffee and head out.

I climb into the truck, letting the grin have me. The old ladies can gossip—heck they are probably planning our wedding by now.

I fire up the engine, Gabby's laugh stuck in my head like a song I don't want to turn off.

She thinks she's one and done.

But I've got a feeling this story's just getting started.

~

That night, after frozen pizza and TV I don't watch, I get ready for bed with my usual routine.

But before lights out, I do what's becoming a nightly habit.

I pray.

Lord, I don't really know what I'm doing here.

I pull the blankets closer to my chin.

Gabby—she's got walls up higher than I've ever seen. She's hurting, though she'd never admit it. Lost her job, feels like she failed.

I turn to my side.

Whatever You want me to do, I'm willing. I'd love to help her see she's not alone. That it's okay to let people care.

I turn back to the other side.

And Lord—I like making her laugh. I like that she pretends to be tough but has the softest heart. So if this is going somewhere, I trust Your timing. If not, I trust that too. Just help me be a good friend.

I breathe.

In Jesus' name, amen.

The apartment is quiet. Just me, the fan, and that peaceful feeling you get from laying something at God's feet.

saturday, february 5th

GABBY

I tell myself I'm only here for honey and tomatoes.

In and out. Quick lap, wave at people I can't avoid, then home—before Mom spots me.

The farmers market's already humming. White tents line the sidewalk, vendors chatting, kids sticky with kettle corn. I breathe in cold air, woodsmoke, fresh bread. Against my better judgment, my shoulders drop.

There are days this town feels too small—every eyeball remembering every dumb thing I've done. But days like this? Ashen Mills feels like a warm quilt. Today's a quilt day.

And I hate that I love it.

"Morning, honey!" Mrs. Taylor calls, already lifting a sourdough loaf. "For Christie?"

"She didn't send me," I say, accepting it anyway.

She winks. "Tell her it's from my oldest starter."

I pull out a twenty. She waves me off. "You'll do no such thing. Go on."

I tuck the bread in my tote—the one I swore I wouldn't fill—and keep walking.

Halfway to the honey booth, I hear my name.

"Gabby! Wait up!"

I don't have to turn. That voice is becoming dangerously familiar.

Rhett Lawson—full uniform today, badge gleaming in the morning sun, utility belt sitting perfectly on his hips, boots polished despite the dusty market path. That easy stance like the ground steadies under him out of respect.

And oh no. He looks even better in uniform than I remembered. Which should be illegal. Actually, maybe it is, and he just hasn't cited himself yet.

"Morning," he says, falling in step beside me.

"Farmers market patrol?" I ask, gesturing to his uniform, trying to sound casual and not like I'm actively trying not to stare.

"Community outreach," he says with a grin. "Chief likes us visible on busy Saturday mornings. Make sure everyone feels safe buying their honey and artisan soaps."

"How noble of you."

"I do what I can." His radio crackles briefly with some mundane dispatch chatter, and he adjusts the volume without breaking stride. "Besides, I was hoping I'd run into you."

That pulls me up short. "You following me, Officer Lawson?"

I try very hard not to notice how the uniform makes his shoulders look broader. Or how the badge catches the light just right. Or how he somehow makes being on duty look like off-limits in the best possible way.

Focus, Gabby.

"Maybe a little." He hesitates, rubbing his jaw. There's stubble there now—less clean-cut cop, more regular guy underneath the uniform. Somehow more dangerous. "I was hoping I could get your phone number."

"Why?"

"I don't know, Gabby. I like talking to you. Thought maybe we could exchange numbers. You know, in case of emergency. Or boredom."

My brain short-circuits. He *likes* talking to me?

I sigh. "Give me your phone."

His eyebrows shoot up, genuine surprise crossing his face. He fumbles in his pocket—which involves some maneuvering around his duty belt and radio—and the whole thing is adorably flustered for someone who probably wrote three tickets before breakfast.

He finally extracts his phone and hands it over.

I type my number, add my name, and—because I can't help it—stick a heart emoji beside it.

"There. In case we're both so bored that texting is literally our only entertainment."

He grins, pocketing it carefully. "Good to know I'm your last resort."

"Don't flatter yourself. Now help me find honey before I buy more things I don't need."

He points. "Over there. But you definitely need whatever you're about to buy."

"Terrible financial advice."

"I'm a cop, not an accountant."

~

At the honey booth, Emmie pulls me into a hug. "Gabby! So good to see you! I heard you were back in town!"

"For now," I say with a shrug, trying to sound casual. "Just helping my mom with some church stuff. Trying not to cause any major disruptions."

Caleb chuckles, his eyes twinkling with mischief. "Too late for that. Half the town's already talking about you and Officer Lawson over here."

My stomach does a weird flip. "Of course they are. This town needs better hobbies."

Rhett raises both hands, picture of innocence. "What can I say? I'm apparently a magnet for local gossip. It's a gift."

Emmie grins, clearly enjoying this. "You two want to try the new clover blend? It's lighter than last year's batch, a little sweeter. We're pretty proud of it."

She dips a tiny wooden stick into a sample jar and hands it over. I taste it—smooth, sweet, with a subtle floral note—and nod approvingly. "Okay, that's actually really good. Better than the stuff at the grocery store."

"Because it's made with love," Emmie says, pressing a hand to her heart dramatically.

"And actual bees," Caleb adds. "The love part is secondary."

I laugh. "I'll take a jar of this."

As Emmie starts to ring me up, I reach for my wallet, but Rhett is faster—of course he is. He pulls his wallet from his back pocket with practiced ease—probably does this motion a hundred times on shift—and I'm definitely not watching the way his uniform shirt stretches slightly across his shoulders.

Definitely not.

He slides a ten-dollar bill across the counter before I can even find my debit card.

"Keep the change," he says to Caleb.

I blink at him. "You didn't have to do that."

"I know," he says simply, tucking his wallet back with that same easy confidence.

Caleb winks at me. "He's a keeper, Gabby."

"Can't keep someone we're not even dating," I say quickly, probably too quickly.

Emmie and Caleb exchange one of those looks—the kind married couples share when they think they know something you don't.

We say our goodbyes and step back into the sunlit path between booths. I glance down at the honey jar glinting in my tote, then up at Rhett, who's looking way too pleased with himself.

"You really didn't have to pay for that," I say.

"I know," he repeats, with that small, lopsided grin that's somehow more dangerous than the full one. "But I wanted to."

I roll my eyes, but my traitorous mouth betrays me with a smile before I can stop it.

"You know," Rhett says, "my mom used to sell candles at markets like this."

I glance at him, surprised. "Really?"

"Yeah. Back in San Antonio. She was always into something creative—scrapbooking, crocheting, painting Bible verse signs. But candles stuck."

"That's kind of perfect. Everybody loves candles."

"She'd say it's less business, more 'calling.'" He uses air quotes. "Started in our kitchen. I remember she melted wax in this big pot she swore she'd replace. Never did. Whole house smelled like vanilla and oranges for weeks."

I can picture it. "Sounds actually kind of perfect."

He nods. "She's always been creative. My dad loved it too. Built her shelves for her first booth, helped design labels, drove her to every market. He called her 'the boss.'"

"That's really sweet."

"Yeah." His voice drops. "She stopped for over a year after my dad passed. Just couldn't do it without him."

I watch memories play across his face—grief and fondness mixing.

"But she's got this little shop now," he continues, brightening. "Downtown San Antonio. Sells her candles, friends' crafts. Says it's her retirement hobby, but she works more hours than I do."

I nudge his shoulder. "She sounds wonderful."

He glances down. "She is."

There's something about seeing him like this—still in uniform but talking about his family, his past, the soft parts underneath the badge—that does dangerous things to my heart rate.

"How about you?" I tease. "Got a creative side? Secret pottery obsession?"

He laughs. "Not quite. But I make a mean Christmas tree. My sister says I'm obsessive."

"I can absolutely see that."

His grin turns mischievous. "You'll have to visit her shop sometime. She'd like you."

I blink, caught by the sincerity. "You think?"

"Oh, I know. You'd be her favorite—someone who keeps me on my toes."

I shake my head. "You really think you've got me figured out?"

He shrugs. "Not even close. But if I hang around long enough, you might let me try."

Heat creeps up my neck. "Keep dreaming, Officer Lawson."

He bumps my shoulder. "Oh, I plan to."

RHETT

We've been walking for almost an hour. She claims she came for two things. Her tote's now holding cookies, a wooden spoon, a succulent plant, and a crocheted scarf she insists she "might need eventually."

Not that I mind. Watching her drift between booths, laughing with vendors, pretending not to enjoy herself—it's the best part of my shift so far.

I can't remember the last time I laughed this much. Or wanted someone to stick around to see what comes next.

There's something about her—this mix of sharp wit and unexpected warmth—that keeps catching me off guard. The way she rolls her eyes but can't hide her smile. The way she tries so hard not to belong here but fits right in.

Yeah. I'm in trouble.

The sun's higher now, glinting off jam jars and catching in her hair. She looks relaxed in a way I haven't seen before—guard down, walls lowered.

The path opens to the town center. There it is— the old gazebo, slightly crooked, white paint peeling. A local band's set up inside, guitar and fiddle filling the air. Couples sway on the grass under weak winter sun.

"Don't even think about it," Gabby says without looking.

"Think about what?"

She keeps walking, but her mouth twitches. "Whatever you're scheming. That look you get before you do something dumb and charming."

"Dumb *and* charming?" I press a hand to my chest. "You're gonna make me blush, Miss Wallace."

She sighs. "Rhett..."

"See, when you say my name like that, it sounds less like a warning and more like an invitation."

I nod toward the dancers. "Miss Wallace, I believe you owe me a dance."

She stops dead. "You're kidding."

"Would I kid about a legally binding bet?"

"It was not legally binding."

"I was there. There were witnesses. It holds up in court."

Her glare could melt paint, but I catch amusement flickering underneath. She sets her tote on a nearby bench with exaggerated care.

Then, with an Oscar-worthy sigh, she turns and slips her hand into mine. "One dance."

Her fingers are smaller than mine, warm, grip firm—making sure I know this is under protest.

I grin. "Technically you owe me three, but I'll take what I can get."

"Good," she says, though the word doesn't match the faint smile tugging her lips.

I step closer, guiding her toward the edge where other couples dance. The band's fiddler picks up tempo. Laughter drifts around us.

She eyes me warily. "You sure about this, Lawson? You might regret it when I step on your foot."

"Worth the risk."

She hesitates, then lets me pull her in. The moment her palm fits against mine, something in my chest clicks into place.

I rest my other hand lightly at her waist, and she stiffens.

"Relax. You're not being arrested."

"Feels like it," she mutters, but her lips twitch.

We start slow. Just a sway. The grass crunches

under our boots. The band plays something half-country, half-memory.

"You're not terrible at this," I say after a minute.

She lifts a brow. "That supposed to be a compliment?"

"High praise coming from me."

"Mm. I'll try to contain my excitement."

I chuckle, and before she can anticipate it, I spin her under my arm.

She lets out a startled laugh—bright, surprised, completely unguarded. The sound makes me want to do more stupid things just to hear it again.

When she lands back in step, her cheeks are flushed, eyes wide. "Okay, I'm officially shocked. You can actually dance."

"My mom made sure all her kids could. Said it was a life skill."

She laughs, softer this time. Her hand relaxes in mine, and I can feel her easing into this—into us. The crowd fades. The music slows. All I can think about is how right this feels.

When the song winds down, I don't immediately let go. Can't quite make myself.

A strand of hair has fallen across her face, and before I can think better of it—before common sense kicks in—I reach up and brush it gently behind her ear.

She freezes.

The air shifts instantly. Whatever easy thing we had evaporates.

She takes a small step back, clearing her throat, walls slamming into place. "Well, that's one down. Only two more dances to go, right?"

I blink, thrown by the whiplash. A moment ago she was smiling, laughing, relaxed. Now she's retreated.

"Gabby—"

"I should probably get going," she says quickly, turning toward the bench. "Promised my mom I'd be home by noon."

She's lying. I can tell. But I don't push.

"Yeah. Sure. Of course."

She grabs her bag, hoists it onto her shoulder, and gives me a smile that doesn't reach her eyes. "Thanks for... this. The honey. The dance. All of it."

"Anytime," I say, meaning it more than she knows.

She starts to walk away, then pauses, looking back over her shoulder.

"See you around, Officer Lawson."

"See you around, Wallace."

I watch her disappear into the market crowd until I can't see her anymore.

And I'm left standing by the gazebo, wondering what exactly I did wrong and how I can avoid doing it again.

~

Later that night, after finishing my shift—helped Mrs. Patterson carry groceries, broke up an argument between two vendors over parking spots, wrote exactly zero tickets because everyone was on their best behavior—I head home with my head full of questions.

I go through my evening routine on autopilot. Shower. Change into sweats. Check tomorrow's schedule. Pour water I'll forget to drink.

Before lights out, I pray.

Hey, Lord.

The ceiling fan spins slowly.

Ok so, I like her. More than I probably should for knowing her such a short time. But there's something about her—the way she keeps everyone at arm's length, the way she flinches when things get too real. She's hurting, and I can see it even when she tries to hide behind sarcasm.

Pause.

Help me be patient. Help me not push when she needs space. But also... help her see that she's safe. That she doesn't have to keep running. That opening up won't destroy her.

Another pause.

I don't know what she's carrying, Lord, but I can feel the weight of it. Help her know she's not too much or too broken or too anything. Help her believe she's worthy of being loved well—not because of what she does or how she performs, but just because.

I shift, the sheets rustling.

And if I'm supposed to be part of helping her see that, show me how. Give me the right words. The right timing. Help me love her the way You love her—patient and kind and without keeping score.

I breathe.

In Jesus' name, amen.

The apartment stays quiet, but it feels a little less heavy.

I close my eyes and try to sleep, reminding myself that tomorrow's a new day, that God's got a plan even when I don't, that sometimes the bravest thing you can do is just keep showing up.

But before I drift off, I allow myself one small hope: that maybe, just maybe, Gabby's thinking about me too.

sunday, february 6th

GABBY

Early mornings and I have an understanding. I don't love them, and they don't love me back.

I'm halfway through taming my hair when my phone buzzes.

UNKNOWN NUMBER

Morning, Miss Wallace. Hope you're not speeding on the Lord's day.

I smile before I can stop it. Only one person would text that.

GABBY

Define "speeding."

Three dots appear immediately.

RHETT

Anything over five miles above the limit.

I roll my eyes, grinning like an idiot.

GABBY

You realize texting and driving is also illegal, Officer Lawson.

RHETT

Good thing I'm parked in the church parking lot. Early bird gets the good spot.

I shake my head, pulling on a navy dress. He's ridiculous and charming all at once.

RHETT

See you at church, Miss Wallace.
Try not to run any red lights.

GABBY

No promises. Also, there's only one traffic light and it's been broken for three years.

RHETT

Details.

I catch my reflection. Smile plastered across my face. Great. An overly cheerful cop taking up mental real estate on Sunday morning.

~

Ashen Mills Baptist Church doesn't try to impress. Just beige carpet, frayed hymnals and wooden pews that creak.

I slip to my usual spot—three rows from back. The bulletin mentions card-making after service. I try not to groan.

"Is this seat taken?"

Rhett stands there in a dark gray sweater and jeans, hair combed, smile misbehaving.

I glance at my tote occupying the space. "Yes. By my purse."

He nods solemnly, picks it up with exaggerated care, sets it on the floor, then slides in beside me.

The wood sighs. So do I.

"Stalking me again?"

"Civic duty. Sitting with first-time visitors."

"I literally grew up here. Baptized in that pool in the other room when I was twelve."

"Then I'm being neighborly."

"That's not a thing."

"It is now."

Mrs. Dunlap turns around. "Morning! So lovely to see you two together."

"Morning, Mrs. Dunlap." We say in unison.

"You make such a nice couple," she whispers.

"We're not.." I start to say, but she's already turned back.

Rhett's shoulders shake with laughter. I elbow him.

A soft chord floats from the piano up front. Conversations taper off. People settle into their seats with the rustle of bulletins and the creak of old wood.

Pastor Miller—who has looked exactly the same since I was thirteen, complete with the same wire-rimmed glasses and the same slightly-too-short tie—steps up to the stage.

He welcomes everyone with his humble voice. No performance, no show. Just a man who knows his congregation by name and genuinely cares about each one.

He prays like he's talking to someone he knows personally, not reciting lines. "Father, thank You for bringing us together this morning. Thank You for being faithful even when we're faithless, for loving us even when we're unlovable. Help us hear what You want to say to us today. In Jesus' name, amen."

The worship leader—Jerry, who also runs the hardware store during the week—nods, and everyone stands. Mrs. Chen on the piano joins in.

I fumble with the hymnal, out of practice with finding the right page, so I give up and follow the lyrics projected on the slightly-crooked screen at the front. Rhett shifts closer—close enough that our elbows nearly brush, close enough that I can hear him actually singing and not just mouthing the words like most people do.

His voice is nice. Deeper than I expected, steady and sincere.

I try not to notice. And fail completely.

When the last chord fades and we sit back down, Pastor Miller opens his Bible and smiles out at the congregation.

"This morning, I want to talk about encouragement," he says simply. "It's something we don't think about much, but it's oxygen for the soul. We forget how desperately people need it until we see someone start to breathe again because of a kind word."

He talks about small kindnesses. Texts sent at exactly the right time. Invitations extended to people sitting alone. Showing up when it would be easier not to. Reminding people that God still sees them, even when they feel invisible.

He's not particularly eloquent. Doesn't have any clever sermon illustrations or three-point alliteration. But he's sincere, and somehow that hits harder than any polished speech ever could.

"Sometimes," he says, looking around the room, "the smallest act of love can change someone's entire day. Maybe even their life. Never underestimate what God can do with your willingness to show up."

I shift in my seat, suddenly uncomfortable, like

he's speaking directly to me and my commitment issues.

Beside me, Rhett is perfectly still.

After the service ends I barely have time to stand up and stretch before my mom materializes out of nowhere like a church lady ninja.

She's got a stack of children's bulletins tucked under one arm and two crayons stuck behind her ear like decorative accessories. She beams at both of us. "Fellowship hall. Ten minutes. Card-making. It'll be fun!"

"Mom, I didn't actually agree to—"

"Jesus and glitter," she sings cheerfully, like it's a promise and a threat rolled into one. Then she whirls away to intercept a runaway toddler who's making a break for the parking lot.

I look at Rhett. "I could still make a run for it."

He grins. "You could. But then you'd miss out on all that Jesus and glitter your mom promised."

"That's supposed to convince me to stay?"

"Worked on me."

I sigh, defeated. "One hour. That's it. I'm setting a timer."

"Deal."

Rhett falls in step as we head to fellowship hall. Coffee and cookies already drifting through the corridor.

"You really don't like this kind of thing, do you?" he asks.

I shrug. "Crowds, glitter, forced cheerfulness without enough caffeine? It's a lot."

He grins, holding the door. "Guess I'll just have to make it worth your while."

Mom claps her hands. "Alright, everyone! Before we start, thank you for being here. We're not just decorating cards—we're sending love. Real, tangible love. Ink and paper telling someone, 'You are seen. You matter. You're not forgotten.'"

She softens. "Some residents don't get many visitors. Some might not even remember us. But love doesn't need to be remembered to be real. Sometimes the smallest kindness can change everything."

Then she brightens. "Markers, stickers, scissors —everything's on the tables!"

I set my timer for exactly one hour and join the chaos.

RHETT

The room settles into that good kind of hum—paper sliding across tables, scissors snicking through construction paper, little gasps of delight when a sticker peels away clean. Someone's got a worship playlist going low from a speaker in the corner, just loud enough to keep the atmosphere light but not so loud it drowns out conversation and laughter.

I sit at one of the folding tables. Across from me, a kid who can't be more than six is engaged in what appears to be mortal combat with a glue stick. Beside him, Gabby's trying to help without getting permanently adhered to the project herself.

Her hair's fallen out of whatever she attempted this morning—some kind of clip situation that gave up the fight around verse three of the second hymn. A few strands brush her cheek every time she leans over.

She mutters something under her breath about "losing circulation in her fingers" as she struggles with a sticker backing, and I have to bite the inside of my cheek to keep from laughing.

She catches me looking, raises one eyebrow in challenge like she's daring me to say something, then goes right back to helping the kid glue his paper heart.

Within twenty minutes, the kids are over it.

The initial thrill of unlimited stickers and unsupervised glue has given way to wiggling in chairs, stealing each other's markers, and gravitating toward the snack table where someone wisely put out juice boxes.

When the children finally scatter like startled birds toward cookies and chaos, Gabby picks up one of the leftover blank cards, turning it over in her hands thoughtfully. "Might as well make one, right? Since I'm here and covered in glue anyway."

"Might as well," I agree, grabbing a card too.

The truth is, I'd sit here making cards all afternoon if it meant staying near her, watching the way she concentrates when she thinks no one's looking, the way her defenses come down when she's focused on something other than keeping people at arm's length.

She writes quickly, neat and deliberate, like she's thought about what she wants to say. I'm slower, printing the words carefully so they don't tilt across the page.

YOU ARE LOVED,
EVEN ON THE HARD DAYS.

When I glance up, she's watching me. "Your handwriting is surprisingly good," she says softly, like it genuinely surprises her.

I grin, leaning back slightly. "Occupational hazard. Comes with writing a lot of tickets. People need to be able to read what they're being cited for."

"And notes asking speeding women out to dinner," she adds, lips twitching.

"Hey," I murmur, lowering my voice just enough that it feels like we're sharing a secret in this room full of people, "for the record—you're the first woman I've ever slipped a note to."

Her pen stills mid-stroke. She looks up, and for a second it's just the two of us in this noisy fellowship hall full of paper hearts and half-eaten cookies and children running wild.

"You expect me to believe that?" she asks, teasing but with something gentler underneath.

I hold her gaze. "You don't have to. But it's true."

She shakes her head slowly, pretending to focus on her card again, though her smile's absolutely giving her away.

"What does your card say?" I ask.

She hesitates, then tilts it so I can read.

Jesus loves you.

Simple. Honest. Perfect.

"That's better than mine," I say.

She looks up, startled. "What? No it's not."

"Yours feels like something someone genuinely needs to hear. Mine's just...nice."

Her smile flickers. "Yeah, well..." She pauses, looking down at the card. "Maybe I need to hear it too."

Something in my chest tightens at that admission, at the vulnerability she just handed me without meaning to.

I slide my finished card onto the growing pile in

the center of the table and lean back. "We make a pretty good team, you know."

"Don't push it, Officer Lawson."

I grin. "Worth a shot."

I reach into one of the supply bags under the table, hunting for more stickers for my second card, but my hand lands on something else instead. When I pull it out, three little vials clink together in my palm—metallic silver, red, and one that can only be described as aggressively, violently pink.

Glitter.

Before I can even comment on my discovery, Gabby freezes mid-marker stroke, eyes going wide. "Don't even think about opening those."

I grin, rolling the tiny pink tube between my fingers. "You know, I don't think I've ever met a woman who doesn't like glitter."

"That's because you've never had to clean it out of your hair for three weeks," she fires back, already reaching across the table for it. "Or your car. Or find it in places glitter has no business being."

"Oh, come on," I tease, holding it just out of her reach. "A little sparkle never hurt anybody."

"Rhett..." Her voice has that warning tone.

"Relax," I say, laughing as she lunges slightly across the table. "It's contained. I'm not going to—"

"Give it here before you cause a disaster."

Her fingers graze my wrist as she tries to grab it. She's close—close enough that I can smell whatever vanilla-something she uses in her hair, close enough to see the flecks of gold in her eyes when she glares up at me with mock fury.

"Give. It. Here."

"Make me," I whisper, just to see what she'll do.

Her eyes widen—half shock, half challenge—and in that split second of distraction, my thumb slips on the lid just as her hand reaches for the vial.

The glitter explodes.

And I mean *explodes*.

A cloud of hot pink glitter bursts out like a tiny firework, showering everything within a three-foot radius. It's everywhere—our hands, our shirts, the table, the kids' half-finished cards, probably in our lungs.

Gabby gasps, eyes going wide as she looks down at herself, then at me, then at the carnage we've created.

"You did not..."

"Oh, I definitely did," I say, trying and completely failing to brush some of the glitter off my sweater. "Completely by accident, I swear."

She stares at me for a long moment, glitter literally sparkling on her cheek, in her hair, on her eyelashes.

And then she snorts.

An unwilling, genuine laugh that spills out before she can stop it, her hand flying up to cover her mouth as her shoulders shake.

That's when Christie appears out of absolutely nowhere, hands on her hips, voice somewhere between maternal disappointment and reluctant amusement.

"Rhett Lawson," she says, using his full name like a weapon. "And Gabriella Wallace. Would either of you like to explain why it looks like a unicorn exploded on my fellowship hall table?"

Gabby's face goes crimson. "It was him! He opened it!"

I hold up both hands in surrender. "Technically, ma'am, it was the laws of physics. And maybe slight operator error."

Christie sighs deeply, pinching the bridge of her nose like she's praying for patience. "You two are cleaning this up. Every single speck. And I mean *every speck*. I don't want to be finding glitter in this carpet until Christmas."

"Yes, ma'am," I say automatically, because you don't argue with Christie Wallace.

"Every. Single. Speck." She gives us one last look then turns toward the door. "And don't think I didn't see you laughing, Gabriella."

When the door swings shut behind her, the silence lasts about three seconds before breaking into quiet laughter.

Gabby leans forward, head in her hands, shoulders shaking. "You are an absolute menace to society."

"Technically," I say, grabbing the roll of paper towels from the supply table, "you're an accomplice. You grabbed for it."

"Because you were about to weaponize glitter!"

"In my defense, I didn't realize the lid was so flimsy."

The laughter lingers as we wipe down ourselves and the surfaces. Gabby breaks out a vacuum from the closet and throw away all of the glimmering paper towels.

"That's about as good as it's going to get." She says, putting the vacuum away.

Here," I say, noticing a streak of hot pink shimmering in her hair near her temple. I reach out before I can think better of it, before my brain can catch up with my hand. "You've got a chunk of it right here."

I brush my thumb lightly along her temple, barely touching, just enough to dust away the glob of the glitter.

She goes completely still. Her breath catches audibly.

Then she swallows, reaches up with a slightly shaky hand. "You missed some too," she says, voice a little quieter than before.

She presses the paper towel to my jaw, ostensibly brushing glitter away, but her hand lingers. Her fingertips graze the stubble I didn't bother shaving this morning because it's Sunday and I was running late.

The room's quiet now. Everyone else has cleared out—kids gone home, other volunteers probably in the kitchen cleaning up. Just us, a table covered in pink devastation, and the distant drip of the kitchen sink.

We're too close now. Close enough that I can see the faint freckles scattered across her nose like stars.

"Gabby," I say, her name landing quiet in the space between us.

She looks up, and for a second I forget how to form coherent thoughts.

Then she blinks, steps back like the floor just reminded her where she is and what we're doing. "You missed a spot," she says quickly, too brightly, tossing the paper towel at my chest.

I catch it automatically, trying to hide the grin tugging at my mouth. "Yeah," I murmur, watching her grab her tote bag and head for the door like the building might be on fire,

She pauses at the doorway, looking back. "Thanks for...making this less terrible than I thought it would be."

"Anytime, Gabby."

She smiles, then disappears into the hallway.

I look down at the pink glitter coating my hands and probably my entire future, and think to myself that I'd clean up a thousand glitter explosions if it meant more moments like this.

~

After helping Mrs. Chen carry her keyboard to her car and picking up stray bulletins from the sanctuary, I finally head home.

My apartment feels especially quiet after the noise of the morning. But I go through my Sunday routine. Laundry, dishes, a quick sweep followed by an equally as quick mop. I take a little extra time on the bathroom and then I clean out the fridge and sort through the leftovers that I took home from the station.

I sit down to at my desk to catch up on work emails, but my mind is too distracted. A certain someone covered in glitter has me thinking to0 much.

So, I pray.

Lord, today was...good. Really good. Making cards with her, the glitter disaster—I can't remember the last time something felt that easy, although a bit chaotic. But I also know she's skittish. And I don't want to push her, don't want to rush this, but I also don't want to miss whatever You might be doing here.

A pause.

She made a card today that said "Jesus Loves You". I think maybe she needed to hear that herself. So whatever

I'm supposed to be for her—friend, something more, whatever—help me make sure she knows she's seen. That she matters. That she's not alone, even when she feels like she is.

I take a breath.

And that Jesus loves her, amen.

Whatever's happening with Gabby Wallace, whether it's friendship or something more, I'm just going to keep showing up.

And trust that God knows what He's doing, even when I don't.

monday, february 7th

GABBY

Monday afternoon greets me with the best kind of ambition, absolutely none.

I'm buried under my favorite quilt, surrounded by empty chip bags, half-melted cookie dough ice cream. The TV blinks through another Netflix episode I don't love.

But it's loud enough to drown out my spiraling thoughts. That's the goal.

My phone buzzes. Tara's name flashes—my best friend.

I debate ignoring it. But curiosity wins.

I swipe to answer. Her face fills the screen, cheeks flushed, eyes sparkling.

"Guess what!" she squeals.

I squint, pushing hair from my face. "You finally

learned to poach an egg without setting off the fire alarm?"

"Better!" She thrusts her left hand toward the camera.

A diamond blinds me through the screen.

"Oh, no. You didn't."

"I did!" she shrieks, laughing and crying. "Gabs, look at it! It was perfect! Our song playing, lights off except candles, this whole speech about me being his forever home—Gabs, I almost passed out!"

She flips back to her face, eyes shining. "Can you believe it? I'm getting married!"

"Wow." I force my face into excitement that hopefully doesn't look like I swallowed something sour. "That's incredible. Really. I'm so happy for you."

And I am. Tara deserves this. They're perfect together.

But my stomach just dropped two floors.

She keeps talking—venues, dates in the fall, honeymoon plans, her mom's tears, Derek's parents helping pay.

I keep nodding. "That's amazing!" "You'll be the most beautiful bride!" While staring at that diamond mocking me.

It's everything she's dreamed about.

Everything I thought I'd be close to by now.

"So? How are you?" she asks. "How's the home-town visit?"

I sit straighter, shoving the blanket off, doing my best functioning-adult impression. "Good! Everything's actually great. Really great."

"See! I told you going home for a bit would be good! Sometimes you just need to reset."

I laugh like I agree, like I'm not covered in ice cream and existential dread. "Yeah, totally. You were right."

We talk a few more minutes—she shows me the ring from every angle, I make cooing noises, she promises to send over dates for dress shopping.

When she hangs up, I drop the phone and stare at the ceiling.

The water stain from 2003 stares back.

I fake a gag. "Ugh. Love. Gross."

But I'm lying.

That's what it's been like. All my friends getting engaged, married, houses, babies.

Like the world's sprinting in a race I didn't know we were running, and I'm still looking for my shoes.

The show on TV flickers to the next episode— another impossibly attractive couple falling madly in love in thirty minutes or less, no complications, no student loans, no one gets laid off.

I mute it, sink deeper into the couch cushions, and pull the blanket up to my chin like armor.

I tell myself I'm fine. That this is just temporary. That I just need some time to figure things out, regroup, make a plan. That I'm not jealous of Tara's fairy-tale proposal or anyone else's seemingly perfect life that looks shinier and easier than mine.

But as the spoon scrapes the bottom of the empty carton with a sad, hollow sound, I realize something I really hate admitting even to myself, even here alone on this couch.

Maybe it's not Valentine's Day I'm actually avoiding. Maybe I'm not afraid of love.

Maybe I'm afraid I'm not capable of it.

That there's something fundamentally broken in me that makes me unlovable, un-choosable, the person everyone leaves eventually.

Maybe that's why I keep everyone at arm's length with sarcasm and eye rolls.

Safer that way.

I set the empty bowl on the night stand and close my eyes, letting the Netflix episode play on mute, washing over me in silent, judgmental waves.

RHETT

Monday mornings in Ashen Mills don't move fast.

The town wakes slow—coffee first, conversation second. By eight, Main Street's alive with shop doors opening, old truck engines, the steady hum of normal.

I'm parked at the corner by the pharmacy, finishing my second coffee, watching the world wake up.

Dispatch crackles. "Unit three, check on a noise complaint on Willow Street."

I sigh, tossing my cup. "Ten-four. On my way."

The "noise complaint" is a grown man practicing drums in his garage. More enthusiasm than skill. His wife apologizes before I fully exit the cruiser. The man looks like he wants to vanish.

Next call's a loose dog—Biscuit the golden retriever, third escape this month. I find him two blocks away, investigating trash cans. He comes when called, tail wagging, completely unrepentant.

After that, a stalled car near the diner. Dead battery. I help jump it, make sure she's good, wave off her tip attempt.

Nothing dramatic. Nothing dangerous. Just small-town maintenance—the kind that used to sound boring and now feels grounding. Important in a different way.

Still, by shift's end at five, the day feels heavier than it should.

Maybe it's the quiet. Maybe it's that everyone I talked to had someone waiting at home.

And I've got an empty bungalow and a fridge full of leftovers.

By six, I'm home. Small but mine, clean and quiet, exactly as I left it. I drop my badge on the counter, toe off boots, open the fridge to survey options.

Leftovers or takeout. Again.

I grab the meatloaf, heat it in the microwave, then eat standing at the counter while staring out the window.

I finish eating, rinse the dish, migrate to the couch. I flip on the TV more for noise than anything. Some basketball game hums background. I'm not watching. My phone's on the coffee table, screen dark. I keep glancing at it like it might spontaneously do something interesting.

I tell myself I'm checking for dispatch updates.

But if I'm honest, I'm half hoping for a text from Gabby.

Which is stupid. We've barely known each other a week. We've hung out a handful of times, mostly in group settings except that supply run.

But somewhere between her sarcastic commentary and that laugh of hers, she got lodged in my head and won't leave.

I lean back, running a hand through my hair, exhaling long.

"Get a grip, Lawson. You're not sixteen."

Still, I reach for the phone, thumb hovering over her name.

I could text something casual. Breezy. No pressure.

Hey, still finding glitter in weird places? Found some in my coffee this morning.

But I don't send it.

What if she doesn't respond? What if she thinks I'm clingy? What if I'm reading this entire thing wrong and she's just being polite because her mom keeps throwing us together?

I set the phone down harder than necessary and stand, suddenly restless.

I cross to the window, stare at the quiet street.

This is what I wanted when I left Houston, isn't it? Peace. Steady, predictable rhythm. Somewhere quieter, gentler, where I wasn't constantly bracing for the next terrible call.

So why does it suddenly feel so empty?

I turn off the TV, let the silence settle heavy, tell myself I'm fine. That I like being alone. That I chose this life deliberately, for good reasons.

That solitude and loneliness aren't the same thing.

But when I finally head to bed around ten, after mindlessly scrolling my phone for an hour, the truth sits heavy in my chest.

The quiet that used to feel like peace—like relief from Houston's constant noise—now just feels lonely.

The apartment that used to feel like a fresh start now feels empty.

And I keep thinking about Gabby's laugh, the way her face lit up helping those kids make cards, how real she is even when trying so hard to seem tough.

I lie there in the dark, hands behind my head, and pray before I can overthink it.

Lord, I don't really know what I'm doing. Once again.

The ceiling fan spins slowly.

Help me be patient. Help me not push when she needs space. But also... help her see that she's safe. That she doesn't have to keep running. That opening up won't destroy her.

I breathe.

In Jesus' name, amen.

tuesday, february 8th

GABBY

The Stable on a Tuesday night isn't busy, but it's not empty either. It's that comfortable hum of conversation and clinking glasses, the scent of fried food and old wood mixing with beer and peanut shells on the floor, and the faint twang of a country song playing through a speaker that probably predates me by a solid decade.

I slide onto a stool at the bar, the leather cracked just enough to tell a few stories of its own. The wood's worn smooth from years of elbows and spilled drinks, and there's a gouge near the edge that legend says came from a bar fight in '92. Knowing this town, it's probably true.

"Diet Coke with lime," I tell the bartender.

Talyn—who I went to high school with and

who's made a full career out of being chronically unimpressed by everything and everyone—doesn't even look up from the glass he's drying. He's got that same bored expression he's worn since sophomore year, dark hair falling into his eyes, tattoos creeping up both forearms. He was the kid who showed up to prom in a leather jacket and left early. Now he's the guy who makes the best Old Fashioned in three counties and remembers every regular's drink order without trying.

He slides my Diet Coke across the bar with practiced precision. "Your mother called," he says flatly, like he's delivering news about the weather.

I groan, catching the lime before it bobs away in the fizz. "Are you serious? When?"

"Twenty minutes ago. Said she won't make it to dinner tonight. Church emergency." He makes air quotes around 'emergency' with completely deadpan delivery. "Something about tablecloths being the wrong shade of pink."

I let my forehead thunk against the bar. "I'm changing my name. Moving to a different state. Maybe a different country."

"Won't help." He tosses the towel over his shoulder. "Your mom would still find you. She's got that mom radar." He pauses, the corner of his mouth twitching. "Don't shoot the messenger."

"Too late. You're complicit." But I'm smiling despite myself.

He smirks—barely, just the tiniest shift in expression—and disappears down the rail to help another customer.

I stir the straw through melting ice, the fizz popping against my lip as I take a sip. I was actually looking forward to tonight. Nothing fancy—just burgers and catching up with Mom. She's been running herself ragged planning the Hearts and Hands event, coordinating volunteers, ordering supplies, managing the emotional labor of an entire congregation. I figured maybe she'd like a break, a chance to just be mom instead of Christie Wallace, Event Coordinator Extraordinaire.

Turns out, not even my own mother wants to hang out with me tonight.

I take another sip and glance around, letting the familiar comfort of The Stable wash over me.

The place looks exactly the same as it did when I was in high school. Half restaurant, half honky-tonk, with Christmas lights strung year-round and neon beer signs casting everything in shades of blue and gold. You could get a pulled pork sandwich at noon and a broken heart by midnight. The mechanical bull sits silent in the corner, waiting for Friday night when the real crowds show up and someone inevitably tries to impress a date.

Every table is filled with people I know or at least know of: Mrs. Garcia from the elementary school, grading papers over a basket of fries. A couple of the old football guys—now coaching Little League and sporting dad bods—reliving their glory days. Hannah from the boutique, with her book club, laughing so loud I can hear her from here.

This town is a quilt—stitched together by stories that never fade, patterns that repeat, warmth that wraps around you whether you want it to or not.

I'm halfway through my drink, contemplating whether to order actual food or just go home and raid my parents' fridge, when a flash of movement catches my eye.

Down at the other end of the bar, a man in uniform leans against the counter, waiting for a to-go bag. Even from here, his posture is familiar—relaxed but alert, the kind of stance that comes from years of training. So is the easy laugh he gives Talyn when the bartender makes some dry comment about the police department keeping him fed.

Rhett Lawson.

Of course. Because apparently, I can't go anywhere in this town without running into him.

My stomach does that annoying flutter thing I've been trying really hard to ignore for the past week. I tell it firmly to stop.

It doesn't listen.

He thanks Talyn, grabs the plastic bag, and turns to leave—but then his gaze sweeps the bar and lands directly on me.

For a second, neither of us moves. Recognition flickers across his face, followed immediately by that smile. The one that always looks a little too easy, a little too confident, like he's never met a situation he couldn't charm his way through.

The one that makes my pulse do stupid things.

I glance down at my straw like it's suddenly the most fascinating object in the entire world. Maybe if I don't make eye contact, he'll just leave. Go home. Eat his dinner. Let me wallow in peace.

No such luck.

Next thing I know, boot steps are heading my direction, and then he's sliding onto the stool beside me like it's the most natural thing in the world. Like we planned this. Like we're friends who meet up at bars on Tuesday nights.

"Hey, Miss Wallace," he says, setting his takeout bag on the counter. That smile's still there, warm and genuine. "Small town."

"Feels smaller every day," I mutter into my Diet Coke.

He doesn't leave. Doesn't make excuses about his food getting cold or having somewhere to be. Just sits there, comfortable in the silence, like he's got all the time in the world.

"You eating?" he asks after a moment, nodding toward my empty hands.

"I was supposed to," I say, lifting my glass in a mock toast. "Got stood up by my own mother.

Apparently, pink tablecloths are more important than her only daughter."

That gets a real laugh out of him. The kind that reaches his eyes and makes the corners crinkle. "By your mom? Should I issue a citation? Abandonment? Emotional distress?"

"Both. Add reckless endangerment to my mental health while you're at it."

He's grinning now, full dimples on display, and it's dangerously close to unfair. He reaches for the plastic bag, tearing it open with easy movements. "Well, I happen to have more food here than any one person should attempt to eat." He opens the takeout container between us with a flourish—fried chicken that smells incredible, mashed potatoes drowning in gravy, biscuits glistening with butter, green beans that are probably the healthiest thing on the plate. "And you look like someone who could use a biscuit."

I raise an eyebrow, fighting the smile that wants to break free. "You trying to bribe me with carbs, Officer Lawson?"

"Just enforcing the town's hospitality laws, ma'am." He nudges the container closer, eyes twinkling with mischief. "It's actually a misdemeanor to let a lady go hungry when you've got perfectly good fried chicken available. Section 4, subsection B of the Ashen Mills code."

"You're making that up."

"Maybe." He pushes a clean fork toward me.

The corners of my mouth twitch despite my best efforts. "You're ridiculous."

"And you're stalling." He picks up a biscuit, tears it in half, the steam rising between us. "Come on, Wallace. I know you want to."

He's right. I do. Not just because I'm hungry—though I am—but because sitting here with him feels easy in a way I wasn't expecting. Like maybe I don't have to have my guard up quite so high. Like maybe I can just...be.

"Fine," I say, reaching for the fork. "But only because I'm starving and those biscuits look amazing."

"Whatever helps you sleep at night."

And just like that, dinner for one turns into dinner for two.

~

We clear the to-go containers—and by clear, I mean we absolutely demolish them. Turns out I was hungrier than I thought, and Rhett's right, those biscuits were amazing. The mashed potatoes weren't bad either. Okay, fine, I ate most of them.

I sit back on my stool, pleasantly full—not just from the food, but from the company. The conversation flowed easy, punctuated by laughter. We talked about nothing important. The best and worst foods at The Stable, his most ridiculous calls this week, my complete inability to understand my parents' TV remote situation.

I hadn't realized how long it'd been since dinner conversation felt this effortless.

Across the room, the band finishes setting up on the small stage in the corner—local guys I vaguely recognize from high school, now sporting beards and wedding rings. The lead guitarist taps the mic twice, and feedback squeals briefly before settling. When the first chords of an upbeat country song spill through the room, the dance floor starts to fill.

I recognize the song immediately—something I grew up hearing at every county fair, every summer bonfire, every Friday night that mattered.

I glance back at Rhett.

He's already looking at me with that expression I'm starting to know too well. Mischief and confidence mixed together, equal parts dangerous and impossible to resist.

"Let's go," I say immediately, already pushing back from the bar.

He grins, leaning back against the bar all relaxed charm and trouble. "Leaving so soon, Miss Wallace?"

"No." I stand, crossing my arms, chin lifted. "I'm just getting the second dance over with before you can make it weird."

His grin widens, slow and infuriating and way

too pleased with himself. "Ah, I see. Funny thing—I'd almost forgotten about our little bet."

"Liar. You've been waiting for this all week."

"Maybe." He stands too, and suddenly he's right there, close enough that I have to tilt my head back to meet his eyes. Close enough that I can smell soap and his aftershave. "But since you reminded me," he says, voice dropping lower, "seems rude not to make good on it."

He holds out his hand, palm up, waiting.

For a second—just one suspended, dangerous second—neither of us moves. The laughter and music and clinking glasses blur into background noise. It's just him and me and that outstretched hand and a choice I know I should probably think harder about.

Then I sigh, roll my eyes with as much dramatic flair as I can muster, and put my hand in his.

"I don't want to do this," I mutter.

"And yet here you are." His fingers close around mine, warm and steady and entirely too confident.

RHETT

She rolls her eyes like she's doing me the biggest favor in the world, but her fingers tighten just slightly when I lead her forward. She's pretending this doesn't matter—like it's just another box to check off her list, another obligation fulfilled—but her pulse gives her away. I can feel it, quick and alive, thrumming against my palm where our hands connect.

The floorboards creak beneath our feet as we step into the open space. Couples shift around us, swaying and laughing, boots thudding softly against wood worn smooth by decades of dancing. The song's upbeat enough to keep things light and fun, but slow enough that I can still pull her in close.

She mutters something under her breath about how ridiculous this is, her tone half-exasperated, half... something else.

I grin, guiding her into the first turn. "You say that every time, but you keep saying yes."

Her eyes flash up at me, hazel catching the neon light from the bar. "Don't flatter yourself, Lawson."

"Oh, I don't need to," I tease, keeping my voice low, just for her. "You're already blushing enough for both of us."

She scoffs, but her cheeks betray her immediately, pink rising fast and spreading down her neck. She looks away, pretending to study the stage lights with intense concentration, but I catch the corner of her mouth twitching.

She's fighting a smile. And losing.

The music picks up a little, and I take the lead—nothing fancy, just easy movements, guiding her through a few simple turns. She follows instinctively, like her body remembers even though her brain's still throwing up protests. Even though she's trying really hard not to enjoy this.

But I can tell she is. It's in the way she leans into the turns just slightly, the way her shoulders have dropped from their defensive position, the way she's stopped looking at her feet and started looking at me.

For a while, it's just movement. Just her hand in mine and the rhythm of boots on worn wood and the warmth of her waist under my other hand. The neon lights from the bar catch in her hair every time she turns, turning the soft brown into threads of gold and amber.

She looks up at me once, eyes shining with something I can't quite name, and I swear the air shifts between us.

God, how is this possible? How is it I've known this girl for eight days and it feels like I've known her a lifetime? Like I've been waiting for her without even knowing it?

There's something about her—she's chaos

wrapped in a sundress and sarcasm, sharp edges barely hiding the softness underneath.

And somehow, impossibly, she feels like home.

The song starts to slow halfway through, the tempo easing into something gentler, more intimate. The fiddle softens. The guitar mellows. And I don't let go.

She doesn't either.

Our steps fall into sync like they've been practiced for years instead of minutes. Like we've done this dance a hundred times before in some other life.

Her hand fits perfectly against mine. Her other hand rests just above my shoulder, fingers barely brushing the back of my neck every time she shifts or turns. Every time it grazes my skin, every nerve in my body seems to notice and file it away as important.

She finally looks up again.

There's a question in her eyes. Uncertainty mixed with something that might be hope. Like she's wondering the same thing I am. How we got here. What this means. Whether I feel it too.

I should say something. Make her laugh. Break the tension before it overwhelms both of us. But the words get stuck somewhere between my brain and my throat, lost in the space between us that feels both too wide and not wide enough.

The song ends too soon.

Way too soon.

Applause ripples across the room, breaking the spell. Reality crashes back in—the noise, the crowd, the fact that we're standing in the middle of The Stable on a Tuesday night with half the town watching.

She steps back first, just slightly, and brushes her hair behind her ear. Her eyes drop to the floor, and I can practically see the walls going back up brick by brick.

"Well," she says after a beat, voice determinedly casual, "two down. One to go."

I shove my hands into my pockets to keep from reaching for her again. To keep from pulling her back and asking for just one more song. "Guess I'll have to find a reason for number three."

She glances over her shoulder as she turns to leave, a smirk tugging at her lips even though her eyes are still soft. "Don't strain yourself, Officer."

And just like that, she's gone—walking back toward the bar, back behind those walls she builds faster than I can climb them.

I stay where I am, watching her retreat, watching her slip back onto that barstool and reach for her drink like nothing just happened.

The band rolls into the next song, louder and faster, and the room fills with laughter and movement again. Couples spin past me. Someone whoops. The bass thumps through the floorboards.

But I'm not listening. I'm not watching the band or the crowd.

Eight days.

That's all it's been since I pulled her over on Highway 77.

Eight days, and she already feels like someone I've been waiting on for a long, long time.

And maybe that's the problem—maybe that's what scares me—because for the first time in a while, in a very long while, I don't want to wait anymore.

I want to know what happens next.

I want to know if she feels it too.

I want to know if maybe, just maybe, God brought me to Ashen Mills for more than just peace and quiet and a fresh start.

Maybe He brought me here for her.

wednesday, february 9th

GABBY

I'm power-walking through Piggly Wiggly like I'm in a grocery-themed triathlon, cart wheels squeaking protest with every turn.

Mom's list is crumpled in my hand, written in her signature half-cursive, half-hieroglyphic style that I swear she does on purpose just to test my decoding skills. It reads like a culinary dare:

Flour
Sugar
Chocolate chips (semi-sweet AND milk chocolate)

Two kinds of sprinkles (don't forget the heart-shaped ones!)
Baking powder
Vanilla extract

I squint at the next item.

Canned pineapple

"Who even needs canned pineapple for a church event?" I mutter, tossing it into the cart anyway because arguing with Mom's grocery lists is a battle I learned to stop fighting years ago.

The store's almost empty—it's mid-afternoon on a Wednesday, that dead zone between lunch and dinner when most normal people are at work. The fluorescent lights hum overhead, and music drones from speakers that haven't been updated since the '90s. I should be in and out in fifteen minutes, tops.

I'm rounding the corner toward the baking aisle, trying to decipher whether Mom wrote "cornstarch" or "cornbread" while simultaneously not crashing into the endcap display of Valentine's candy—because of course there's Valentine's candy everywhere, even in the baking aisle—when fate decides to have a little fun at my expense.

There's a solid *thunk*, followed by a sharp,

theatrical gasp that could probably be heard in the next county.

"Oh my stars!"

My head snaps up.

And there she is—Mrs. Carmichael—clutching her pearls like I've just committed a felony, sitting in the captain's seat of her electric mobility scooter with the kind of wounded dignity usually reserved for soap opera actresses.

I freeze, hands still gripping my cart. "Mrs. Carmichael, I am *so* sorry, I didn't see—"

"You ran me clean over!" she declares, her voice loud enough to send nearby shoppers scattering like startled pigeons. A woman with a toddler actually speed-walks away from the scene.

"I bumped your wheel," I say quickly, holding up both hands in surrender. "Barely. I didn't even...your scooter didn't move, I swear..."

She points a perfectly manicured finger at a spot on her scooter's bumper. "You see this? You see this dent?"

I squint at the alleged damage. "Mrs. Carmichael, that's...that's a sticker. From the manu- facturer."

She gasps like I've personally insulted her entire lineage, three generations back. "You've got some nerve, Gabriella Wallace! Absolute *nerve*! I could've been paralyzed from the knees down!"

"You're...you're sitting down," I point out

weakly, already knowing this is a losing battle. "And your scooter only goes four miles per hour. Maximum."

"How dare you minimize my trauma!" She clutches her chest now, the pearls apparently insufficient for the level of drama required. "I've been assaulted! In broad daylight! In the Piggly Wiggly!"

The deli counter clerk hurries over, hands raised like he's approaching a hostage situation. "Now, now, Mrs. Carmichael, I'm sure it was just an accident—"

"Accident? *Accident?*" She swivels to face him, eyes blazing with righteous fury. "This girl has been trouble since high school! Do you remember the homecoming parade? She set the entire float on fire!"

"That was a fog machine malfunction!" I protest, my voice climbing higher than I'd like. "The fire marshal cleared me! It was in the paper!"

"She's lying again! Just like she lied about the principal's office! And the swimming pool incident!"

"I was *twelve*!"

"Troublemaker then, troublemaker now!" She's really getting into it now, warming to her subject like a preacher at a tent revival. "Mark my words, this girl is a menace to society!"

I press both hands to my forehead, trying to remember the breathing exercises my therapist taught me. "Mrs. Carmichael, I promise you, I barely touched—"

She whips out her phone like it's a weapon. "I'm calling 911!"

I blink. Surely she's joking. "You're...what?"

"You heard me, young lady! Reckless endangerment by shopping cart! Hit and run! I'm pressing full charges!" She's already dialing, phone pressed to her ear with trembling fingers that seem perfectly functional despite her claims of injury.

"Ma'am, that's not...there's no such thing as...”

"Don't you 'ma'am' me, Gabriella Wallace. I know your tricks. I know your whole family's tricks. Your mother once sold me a bundt cake that was slightly lopsided!"

"What does that have to do with—"

"Chaos! Your whole bloodline is chaos!"

By now, the store is practically silent except for Mrs. Carmichael's dramatic narration into the phone. A stock boy has abandoned his cart to watch. The cashier is filming on her phone—great, this'll be on the town Facebook page within the hour.

Five minutes later, Mrs. Carmichael is still on the phone—now insisting she can't feel her left leg and might need life-flight to Dallas.

I'm approximately one forced apology away from losing my entire mind when the automatic doors at the front of the store whoosh open.

And in walks the cavalry.

Well, the cavalry in the form of two paramedics with a stretcher they definitely won't need, followed by...oh no.

Officer Rhett Lawson strides through those doors like he's walking onto a movie set, all calm confidence and clean lines, heading straight toward my personal circle of chaos. He's in full uniform—badge gleaming, utility belt sitting perfectly on his hips.

He's unfairly attractive on a normal day. Right now, backlit by the fluorescent lights and coming to rescue me from grocery store drama? It's borderline devastating.

Our eyes meet across the produce section.

He has the audacity to smirk.

I want to sink through the floor.

RHETT

The call came through dispatch as a "possible injury" at the Piggly Wiggly, and I volunteered immediately because it's a slow Wednesday and I was bored doing paperwork. Plus, any call involving Mrs. Carmichael usually provides entertainment value, if nothing else.

What I wasn't expecting was to walk in and find Gabby Wallace standing in the baking aisle looking like she wants the earth to open up and swallow her whole, while Mrs. Carmichael performs what can only be described as a one-woman show about assault by grocery cart.

"Finally!" she cries, pointing a trembling—but notably steady—hand in my direction. "It's about time the law showed up! Though I must say, this is *highly* inappropriate!"

I stop a few feet away, hooking my thumbs in my belt. "Ma'am?"

She gasps, actually *gasps*, like I've revealed some scandal. "You. You can't possibly be the officer responding to this incident. It's a conflict of interest!"

The paramedics beside me are already trying not to laugh. I can see their shoulders shaking.

I keep my expression carefully neutral. "Conflict of interest? How do you figure that, ma'am?"

Mrs. Carmichael crosses her arms—despite apparently being grievously injured—and lifts her chin triumphantly. "Because you're dating the defendant!"

Gabby makes a sound like a dying cat. "We are *not* dating!"

Her face is the color of a fire truck, and her hands are clenched so tight around her shopping cart that her knuckles are white. She looks mortified and furious and completely flustered.

Man, she's cute when she's embarrassed.

"Ma'am," I say, forcing my voice into something resembling official professionalism even though I'm fighting a grin, "I can assure you, I am not dating Miss Wallace." I crouch down a little, getting closer to Mrs. Carmichael's eye level, and lower my voice to something gentle and reassuring. "But I *am* here to help, and I need to make sure you're okay. That's my job. Sound fair?"

She huffs, unmoved by my attempt at charm. "I've been run over. Mowed down. Nearly killed."

"By a shopping cart?" I keep my tone carefully neutral.

"By a *weaponized* shopping cart," she corrects with absolute conviction. "Wielded by a known troublemaker."

I nod slowly, like this is the most serious thing I've heard all week. "Of course. That's a very serious allegation. We'll need to get a full report." I glance over at the paramedics, who are now actively biting their lips to keep from laughing. "Why don't you let these fine folks check you over—make sure there's no injuries—while I take your official statement? Would that work?"

Mrs. Carmichael's chin wobbles slightly, but her voice softens just a fraction. "Well... I suppose if you insist on being professional about it..."

"That's exactly what I insist on, ma'am," I say, flashing my most reassuring smile—the one I save for elderly ladies and scared kids. "Your safety is my number one priority."

That does it. She practically preens.

"Well, when you put it that way... I suppose I can allow it. But I want it on record that this is highly irregular!"

"Duly noted, ma'am."

Within minutes, she's settled on the paramedics' stretcher—which she absolutely doesn't need but insisted upon—while they go through the motions of checking her vitals and asking about phantom pain. I pull out my notepad, taking her "statement" with appropriate gravity while she describes the "attack" in increasingly dramatic detail.

The whole time, I'm painfully aware of Gabby standing fifteen feet away, trying to be invisible, slowly inching her cart toward the registers. Her face is still pink, her hair's falling out of whatever she tried to do with it this morning, and she keeps glancing at the exit like she's calculating escape routes.

There's something about her in this moment— shoulders squared like she's daring anyone to laugh at her, jaw set in stubborn defiance even though she's clearly mortified—that just knocks the wind straight out of me.

She's funny when she's flustered. Cute when

she's embarrassed. Beautiful when she's trying to be tough.

And as absolutely ridiculous as this entire situation is, there's a part of me—a growing, insistent part—that feels weirdly pleased hearing someone accuse me of dating her.

Even if it's Mrs. Carmichael.

Even if it's in the middle of the Piggly Wiggly.

Even if Gabby looked horrified by the very suggestion.

I shake my head at myself, exhaling quietly. *Get a grip, Lawson.*

By the time Mrs. Carmichael's convinced that her oxygen levels are "acceptable but concerning" and the paramedics have declared her miraculously uninjured—shocking absolutely no one—Gabby's already finished checking out. I watch her load her bags into her cart with quick, efficient movements, head down, trying to make herself small.

She's halfway to the automatic doors when I catch up.

"Hold up, Wallace."

She stops, shoulders tensing, but doesn't turn around. "If you're here to arrest me for assault with a deadly shopping cart, just get it over with."

I step around to face her, fighting a smile. "Not today. But I might need your statement."

She finally looks up, and her eyes flash with that familiar mix of defiance and humor. "My statement is that Mrs. Carmichael has hated me since I was five and dropped my ice cream cone on her shoe at the Dairy Queen. She's been holding a grudge ever since."

I grin. "Sounds like a serious offense."

"Apparently unforgivable."

"Clearly," I say, falling into step beside her as she pushes her cart into the parking lot. The February air is crisp, the sun bright and cold. "But for the record, I didn't see any evidence of reckless endangerment."

"Really?" She glances at me sideways, suspicious. "You're not just saying that because..."

"Because what?"

"Because you..." She trails off, shaking her head. "Never mind."

"No, go ahead." I lean against her car as she opens the trunk. "Because I what?"

She starts loading groceries with more force than necessary. "Because you're weirdly nice to me for reasons I don't understand."

That stops me. "Weirdly nice?"

"Yeah." She doesn't look at me, just keeps transferring bags. "Everyone else in this town sees 'Gabby Wallace, troublemaker.' But you..." She finally glances up. "You don't."

The vulnerability in her voice catches me off guard. For a second, I forget we're standing in a grocery store parking lot. Forget that I'm in uniform. Forget everything except the fact that she thinks I'm nice to her for weird reasons, when the truth is I'm nice to her because I can't seem to help it.

"You want to know what I see?" I ask quietly.

She swallows, nods.

"I see someone who shows up even when she doesn't want to. Someone who helps her mom even when she's complaining about it. Someone who's good with kids and makes people laugh." I pause. "I see someone who's a lot kinder than she wants anyone to know."

Her face flushes pink again, but this time it's different. Softer.

"That's..." She clears her throat. "That's a much better assessment than 'menace to society.'"

"Mrs. Carmichael's wrong about you."

"She's not the only one who thinks that way."

"Then they're all wrong." I say it firmly, meaning every word. "And for what it's worth, I'm glad you bumped her scooter."

She blinks. "Why?"

"Because I got to see you defend yourself against accusations of vehicular assault with a grocery cart. That's not something you see every day." I grin. "Plus, I got to play knight in shining armor. My mom would be proud."

She shakes her head, but she's smiling now—a real smile that reaches her eyes. "You're ridiculous."

"And you're trouble," I counter. "But the good kind."

She holds my gaze for a beat longer than necessary, and something passes between us that makes the cold February air feel irrelevant.

"Hey, Officer Lawson?" she says finally, closing her trunk.

"Yeah?"

She tilts her head, eyes glinting with something halfway between gratitude and mischief. "Thanks for the damage control. And for...what you said."

"Anytime, Miss Wallace." I step back to let her open her driver's door. "Try not to cause any more public emergencies before the week's over, though. My shift ends at five and I'd like to go home on time for once."

She rolls her eyes, but she's still smiling as she climbs into her car. "No promises."

"Somehow, I don't believe you."

She starts the engine, then rolls down her window. "For the record?"

"Yeah?"

"You make a pretty good knight in shining armor. Even if the armor's just a police uniform and the dragon is an elderly woman on a scooter."

Before I can respond, she puts the car in reverse and drives off, leaving me standing in the parking lot grinning like an absolute fool.

I watch her disappear around the corner, then head back to my cruiser, shaking my head.

Nine days.

Nine days since I pulled her over, and she's already completely upended my quiet small-town life.

And the craziest part?

I don't mind. Not even a little bit.

In fact, I'm starting to think maybe this town needed a little chaos.

Maybe I needed it too.

thursday, february 10th

GABBY

My phone buzzes on the couch beside me, interrupting my very important activity of scrolling through job listings I'm not qualified for while eating cereal straight from the box.

> **RHETT**
>
> I need a favor. Can I borrow your expertise today?

I set down the cereal box, intrigued despite myself.

> **GABBY**
>
> Depends on what kind of "expertise" we're talking about...

RHETT

Let's just say I may have
overcommitted.

GABBY

That's vague and concerning. More
info, please.

RHETT

I signed up to bake cookies for
Saturday's event.

GABBY

And the problem is?

RHETT

I don't know how to bake cookies.

I actually laugh out loud at that, alone in my
living room like a crazy person.

GABBY

And you think I do?

RHETT

That's my working theory. You seem
like someone who knows her way
around a kitchen.

GABBY

Based on what evidence?

RHETT

You successfully navigated the Dollar General Valentine's aisle without causing permanent psychological damage. That takes skills.

GABBY

That's terrible logic.

RHETT

My house. 3pm?

I should say no. I should absolutely say no. Going to his house feels like crossing some invisible line we've been carefully dancing around for the past week and a half.

But my fingers are already typing.

GABBY

Fine. But only if I get to take some cookies home.

RHETT

Deal. Assuming we make anything edible.

~

I follow the GPS directions through town, turning onto Main Street where the storefronts transition from the newer strip mall to the old downtown buildings. The hardware store sits on the corner, its red brick facade weathered but solid, the building has been here since before I was born.

I pull into the small parking lot beside it and kill the engine, staring up at the second floor. His apartment. The windows have simple white curtains, and I can see warm light glowing from inside.

There's an external staircase along the side of the building—black metal, slightly rusted at the joints—leading up to a navy blue door. A small landing at the top holds a welcome mat that says *Welcome to the Love Shack* in bold letters.

I roll my eyes so hard it actually hurts, but my mouth tips up anyway despite my best efforts. Of course his mat says that. Of course it does.

I grab my tote bag—packed with vanilla extract, baking powder, and chocolate chips because I absolutely didn't trust him to own the basics—and climb the metal stairs. They clang slightly under my feet, announcing my arrival.

The door is cracked open, and I can hear life happening inside. Music playing faintly in the background—some country song I vaguely recognize. The sound of off-key whistling. An occasional clang like something metal just lost a fight with gravity.

"Please don't be injured," I mutter, pulling open the door and stepping inside without knocking. "Rhett?"

"Kitchen!" he calls back, though in an apartment this size, the kitchen is really just around the corner.

The apartment smells incredible—cinnamon and coffee and that faint clean-laundry scent that only men who actually care about their space somehow manage to pull off. His living room is small but warm, soft gray couch that looks actually comfortable wedged against one wall, a stack of guitar magazines on the coffee table next to a half-finished crossword puzzle, a few framed photos on a narrow shelf showing his family and a golden retriever that could absolutely be his spirit animal.

The whole space is maybe 600 square feet, but it doesn't feel cramped. It feels lived-in. Cozy.

But the kitchen—which is really just a galley-style setup along one wall—looks like a crime scene.

Every single cabinet door hangs open like they're gasping for air. Cookie sheets, mixing bowls in three different sizes, measuring cups, and what looks like an entire arsenal of spatulas cover every available inch of the small counter. A bag of flour is tipped on its side, spilling in a small white snowdrift across the laminate countertop and onto the tile floor.

And in the middle of this beautiful disaster stands Rhett Lawson—black T-shirt that fits him unfairly well, sleeves pushed up to his elbows revealing forearms that should probably be illegal, hair slightly mussed like he's been running his hands through it, whistling off-key while brandishing a wooden spoon like it's evidence in a murder trial.

He turns when he hears me, and that grin spreads across his face—easy, genuine, stupidly attractive. "You came."

"You doubted me?" I set my tote down on the only clear spot of counter I can find—which happens to be approximately two inches wide—and cross my arms, taking in the absolute chaos. "What exactly happened here? Did you get in a fight with your kitchen and lose?"

He glances around like he's seeing the mess for the first time. "Technically, I was testing the equipment. Making sure I had everything I needed."

"By emptying your entire cabinets onto the counter? In a kitchen this size?"

"You never know when you'll need options." He says it so seriously that I can't tell if he's joking.

I shake my head, fighting a smile. "Okay, what exactly were you planning to bake?"

He holds up a recipe card like it's a treasure map he found in an attic. "Chocolate chip cookies. Classic. Can't go wrong."

"That's it? Just chocolate chip?"

He squints at the card, flips it over. "We could also do plain sugar cookies? It says those are 'beginner-friendly.'" He makes air quotes with one hand, still holding the wooden spoon with the other.

The laugh bubbles out of me before I can stop it

—genuine and surprised and absolutely not something I planned to give him.

His entire face lights up. "That's the first time you've laughed at something I said on purpose."

"Don't get used to it." But I'm smiling, and we both know it. I step closer—which in this tiny kitchen means we're practically on top of each other—to survey the damage up close. "Okay, move over. If I'm helping, I'm in charge."

"Yes, ma'am."

I glare at him. "Don't start that again."

He chuckles, and slides aside as much as the small space allows. "You really came prepared," he says, nodding at my tote bag. "Is that—did you bring your own vanilla extract?"

"I didn't trust you to own the basics. Or if you did own them, I didn't trust them to be less than five years expired."

"That's fair. Also slightly insulting, but fair."

As I start pulling ingredients from my bag and organizing the chaos on his limited counter space into something resembling order, he leans against the narrow strip of counter beside me. In an apartment kitchen this small, close enough means *close enough*—I can feel the warmth radiating from his arm, can smell whatever soap or cologne he uses.

He doesn't say anything, just watches—amused, relaxed, comfortable in the silence.

"You're staring," I say without looking up from measuring flour.

"I'm supervising."

"You're in the way."

"Also true." But he doesn't move. Can't move much farther without leaving the kitchen entirely.

And somehow, standing in this tiny apartment kitchen with sunlight streaming through the single window and the smell of sugar and the sound of country music playing softly from his phone on the counter, it hits me how easy this feels.

Too easy.

I shouldn't like this. Shouldn't like the domestic simplicity of baking cookies with him in this cramped space on a Thursday afternoon. Shouldn't like the sound of him humming along to the music, or the quiet rhythm of moving around each other in quarters so close we keep accidentally bumping elbows.

But I do. I like it more than I want to admit.

And that realization scares me more than any speeding ticket ever could.

"Okay," I say, clearing my throat and pushing the thoughts away. "First lesson, you need to cream the butter and sugar together. That's the base for basically everything."

"Cream them?" He looks genuinely confused. "Like...put cream in them?"

"No, you—" I stop, looking at his face. He's grinning. "You're messing with me."

"Maybe a little." He picks up the butter, examining it like it might contain instructions. "But I genuinely don't know what I'm doing, so feel free to assume all my questions are serious."

RHETT

She hums when she concentrates. Soft and unconscious, just barely audible under the music. I don't think she realizes she's doing it, but it might be my new favorite sound in the entire world.

The kitchen looks like a war zone—there's flour on the counter, flour on the floor, flour somehow in my hair. There's a tray of sugar cookies cooling by the window, another batch waiting to go in the oven, and a mixing bowl that's seen significantly better days.

And yet this might be the most fun I've had in months. Maybe years.

Gabby laughs as she tries to scrape sticky cookie dough off the rolling pin. "You're supposed to flour it first, genius. That's literally the entire point of having flour on the counter."

"I did flour it," I protest, though even I don't sound convinced. "Just... apparently not enough."

"You think?" She smirks, brushing past me to grab the flour bag, her shoulder grazing mine in a way that makes me hyperaware of every point of contact.

The kitchen suddenly feels smaller. Warmer. The air thicker.

She pours a generous dusting of flour across the counter, then reaches for the rolling pin still in my hand. "Here," she says, and before I can process what's happening, she's stepping up behind me. Her hands slide over mine, small and warm and deliberate, guiding the rolling pin across the dough. "Light pressure. You don't need to crush it into submission. Just... gentle, even strokes."

"Noted." My voice comes out lower than I meant it to, rougher.

She's so close I can smell her shampoo and feel the warmth of her breath against my neck when she speaks. "You're still using too much pressure."

"Sorry. I'm better at tackling suspects than rolling dough."

"You're terrible at this," she says, hands still covering mine, still guiding the motion.

"Yeah, but I take direction well."

She snorts, and I can feel her smile even though I can't see it. "That remains to be seen."

For a few perfect seconds, we just stay like that—her hands on mine, her body close, the dough rolling out smooth and even. Then she steps back, clearing her throat slightly, and the spell breaks.

But the warmth lingers.

I grin and, without thinking too hard about it, reach for the bowl of pink frosting we made earlier. I dip my finger in, just enough to make her suspicious.

Her eyes narrow instantly. "Don't even think about—"

Too late. I swipe a dot of frosting across the tip of her nose.

She gasps, hand flying to her face. "You did not just—"

"Oh, I absolutely did."

"That's it." She lunges for the spoon, determination in her eyes, aiming straight for my face. "You're going down, Officer Lawson."

The next few seconds are pure, beautiful chaos.

"Got you!" she shouts, triumph lighting up her entire face when a smudge of frosting ends up on my cheek.

"Oh, not a chance." I dodge her next attack, reaching for the spoon she's brandishing like a sword. "That's assault on an officer."

She squeals and takes off around the island,

giggling as she nearly slips on a patch of flour. "You'll never take me alive!"

"Careful," I warn, chasing her with probably too much enthusiasm. "Wouldn't want another 911 call on our record. Mrs. Carmichael would have a field day."

She throws a handful of flour over her shoulder in retaliation, and I charge through the cloud, blind and determined. When I catch her wrist, she gasps, spinning toward me just as I pull her closer.

Momentum does the rest.

Her back hits the counter, my hand still wrapped around her flour-dusted wrist. For a heartbeat neither of us moves. The only sound is her laughter fading into breathless silence and the faint thrum of the country song playing behind us.

We're both covered in sugar and chaos—her hair a wild mess of brown waves, my shirt dusted completely white, both of us breathing hard from laughing and running—but all I can think about is how close she is.

How right this feels.

My eyes catch a streak of frosting at the corner of her mouth, pink against her skin. I reach up without thinking, without asking permission, and brush it away with my thumb.

Then, because I've apparently lost all sense of self-preservation, I lick the frosting off my thumb, holding her gaze the entire time.

She goes completely still.

Her pupils dilate slightly. Her lips part. Her breathing changes.

"Rhett," she whispers, and my name has never sounded like that before. Like a question. Like a dare. Like permission.

I shouldn't. I know I shouldn't. We've been dancing around this for days, and every time we get close, she pulls away. Every time she lets me in, she finds a reason to lock the door again.

But then her gaze flicks to my lips—quick and unguarded and absolutely intentional—and every logical thought in my head evaporates.

"Gabby," I whisper back.

She doesn't pull away. Doesn't make a joke. Doesn't rebuild her walls.

She just looks at me with those hazel eyes, flour dusting her cheek, frosting still at the corner of her smile, and waits.

So I do the only thing I can—the only thing I've wanted to do for days.

I lean in, slow enough to give her a chance to stop me, to push me away, to say no.

She doesn't.

Her breath catches when I'm close enough that our lips almost touch, and when they finally do, it's soft. Tentative at first, testing, learning. She tastes like sugar and vanilla and something uniquely her, and when she sighs against my mouth I feel it in my bones.

I slide my hand from her wrist to her waist, fingers spreading against the curve of her hip, and she grips my shirt like she needs something to anchor her. Her other hand finds its way to my chest, palm flat over my racing heart.

The counter presses against her back, and before I can overthink it, before I can talk myself out of it, I lift her onto it. She gasps slightly—surprise or permission, I'm not sure—and her legs bracket me in, ankles crossing behind me.

For a long, perfect, crystallized moment, there's nothing but this. Her frosting-sweet lips. The warmth of her body against mine. The soft sound she makes when I deepen the kiss just slightly. The way her fingers curl into my shirt like she's afraid I might disappear.

This. This is what I've been waiting for without knowing it.

Then she breaks the kiss, pulling back just enough to breathe, eyes wide and slightly dazed.

She just stares at me like she's trying to memorize this moment, trying to convince herself it's real.

Then I watch it happen. The walls start going back up. The panic sets in. The defenses rebuild brick by brick right in front of me.

She blinks, and the spell shatters.

"I—uh..." She slides off the counter so quickly I

barely have time to step back. Her feet hit the floor, and she's already busying herself brushing flour from her hands, her jeans, anywhere but looking at me. Her voice comes out sharp and rushed, too casual. "We should probably...uh...clean this up before it turns into an actual health code violation."

"Gabby..."

"Where's your broom?" she interrupts, already scanning the corners of the kitchen like she hasn't just kissed me breathless. Like the last five minutes didn't happen.

I drag a hand through my hair, still trying to catch my breath, still tasting sugar on my lips. "Closet by the fridge."

"Right. Perfect." She grabs it like it's a lifeline, like cleaning is suddenly the most important thing in the world.

For a while, all I can do is watch her sweep up the mess, her movements quick and clipped and so carefully controlled. The same woman who was laughing in my arms five minutes ago, who was kissing me like maybe she'd been waiting for it too, now won't even meet my eyes.

Every time I try to help, to get close, she finds a new corner to focus on, a new bowl to rinse, a new surface to wipe down.

So I do what I can—clean the counters, load dishes into the dishwasher, scoop the last batch of dough onto cookie sheets, pretend my chest doesn't ache from how fast everything changed.

The laughter's gone. The easy rhythm we had replaced by careful silence and the clink of dishes and the too-loud ticking of the clock on the wall.

When the last cookie sheet comes out of the oven, she packs a dozen cookies into a plastic container with practiced efficiency, her voice steady but too casual. "These turned out... surprisingly okay. Better than I expected, actually."

"Yeah." My throat feels dry, tight. "Guess we make a good team."

"Guess so." She doesn't look at me when she says it. Won't look at me.

She tucks her hair behind her ear—a nervous gesture I'm starting to recognize—and slings her bag over her shoulder like she's heading out for a quick errand instead of running away from what just happened.

"See you tomorrow," she says, forcing a polite smile that doesn't reach her eyes. "For the event setup."

"Gabby, wait—"

But she's already at the door, already halfway gone.

"Thanks for the cookies," she tosses over her shoulder, and then she's gone—out the door, down the porch steps, into her car before I can think of something better to say. Something that might make her stay.

The door clicks shut with a soft, final sound.

The apartment feels too quiet when she's gone. Too empty.

I lean against the counter, staring at the pristine countertop that was a mess not that long ago, and let out a slow, shaky breath.

I don't know what I did wrong.

All I know is that every single time she lets me in —every time she shows me the real her, the soft parts underneath all that armor—she finds a way to lock the door again.

And I'm starting to wonder if maybe she always will.

friday, february 11th

GABBY

I've convinced myself yesterday didn't happen.

Well, almost.

The problem is, every time I close my eyes, I can still feel his lips on mine. The warmth of his hands on my waist. The way he said my name—half groan, half plea, like I was something he'd been waiting for his whole life.

And then, of course, the way I panicked and ruined everything.

I tell myself it was smart. Logical. Pure self-preservation. I came back to Ashen Mills to *skip* Valentine's Day, remember? To hide from romance and relationships and anything remotely heart-shaped. To eat ice cream and figure out my life in peace.

Instead, here I am—eleven days into February—and I've somehow managed to get myself roped into organizing a Valentine's event, baking cookies with a man who kisses like it should be illegal, and thinking about said man approximately every thirty seconds.

This is literally the opposite of my plan.

The *opposite*.

Except logic doesn't explain why I've been replaying that kiss in my head on a loop since the moment I drove away last night. Or why I woke up this morning with his wooden spoon still in my tote bag and nearly cried over it like some kind of emotional disaster. Or why I keep glancing at my phone like maybe—just maybe—he'll text.

He hasn't.

And that's fine. Totally fine. I probably broke whatever fragile thing was building between us when I ran away like his kitchen was on fire and I was allergic to feelings.

I pull into a parking spot outside Ashen Mills City Hall, kill the engine, and grab the yellow sheet of paper sitting on the passenger seat—my speeding ticket, the one that started this whole ridiculous cascade of events that's somehow led to me kissing a cop in a flour-covered kitchen.

At least I can finally check something off my to-do list. Pay the ticket. Move on. One less thing tying me to him.

Except even as I think it, I know it's a lie. The ticket stopped mattering somewhere around the second dance. Maybe even before that.

Inside, the lobby smells like old paper. The walls are plastered with community event flyers—pancake breakfasts, lost cat notices, Girl Scout cookie sales, and approximately forty-seven different Valentine's Day events I'm actively avoiding.

The irony of my life right now could kill me.

I'm supposed to be *skipping* Valentine's Day. That was the entire plan. Hide. Regroup. Avoid pink hearts and romantic declarations and anything that makes me feel like a failure for being twenty-six and perpetually single.

Instead, I've spent the last week and a half elbow-deep in pink decorations, baking heart-shaped cookies, and slow-dancing with a man who looks at me like I'm not a complete disaster.

I kind of hate how much I don't hate it.

I take a number and wait my turn behind a guy in overalls arguing passionately about a parking ticket he swears he didn't deserve. When the clerk finally waves me forward, I slide the yellow paper across the counter like it's evidence in a trial.

"Hi," I say, forcing a smile. "I'm here to pay this."

She takes it, barely glancing at me before tapping away at her computer. Her name tag reads *Linda* in faded letters, and she looks like the kind of woman who's been running this office since before I was born and knows everyone's business whether they want her to or not.

"Alright," she says, frowning at the screen. "Let's see here... Wallace, Gabriella?"

"That's me."

She types a few more keys, squints at the monitor like it personally offended her, then clicks her tongue. "Well, that's strange."

My stomach dips. "Strange how?"

"It's already been paid."

I blink. Once. Twice. "I'm sorry, what?"

"Yep." She turns the monitor toward me, pointing at a line of text I can barely read from this angle. "Paid in full on Wednesday, February second, at 8:32 a.m."

Wednesday. February second.

I do the mental math, counting backwards through the blur of the past week. That was the morning after he pulled me over. The same day I met him at The Stable. The same day we made that ridiculous bet about the mechanical bull.

The same day he told me that if I won, he'd pay my ticket.

But I didn't win. He did. Six and a half seconds to my pathetic six.

And he'd already paid it anyway. Before the bet even happened.

I stare at the screen, processing this information

while my heart does complicated things in my chest. A slow, involuntary smile tugs at my lips despite my best efforts to stay annoyed.

Of course he did. Of course he paid it before he even asked me out. That's so perfectly, frustratingly, devastatingly *Rhett* that I want to laugh and cry at the same time.

He bet me on something he'd already done. Like he knew I'd lose. Like the whole thing was just an excuse to dance with me.

"Ma'am? Everything okay?" Linda's looking at me with concern now, probably wondering if I'm having some kind of breakdown in her lobby.

"Yeah." My voice comes out softer than I expect, almost wondering. "Yeah, it's fine. Thank you."

She stamps the corner of the paper with more force than necessary and slides it back across the counter. "You're all squared away, then. Have a nice day."

"You too." I tuck the stamped ticket into my bag, my hands moving on autopilot while my brain tries to catch up with what just happened.

Outside, the February air is cold against my flushed cheeks. I pause on the steps of City Hall, looking down Main Street where the police station sits just past the town square, brick and solid and probably containing one infuriating officer who paid my ticket without telling me.

I should be annoyed. He tricked me. He made a

bet he knew he'd win because he'd already done the thing I was betting on.

But I can't bring myself to be mad.

Because somehow, it doesn't feel like a trick or a manipulation or a game. It feels like Rhett Lawson being exactly who he is. The kind of man who pays a stranger's ticket and then turns it into a reason to make her smile.

And that—*that*—is what scares me most of all.

Not the kiss. Not the feelings I'm definitely not having. But the fact that he's exactly the kind of good I've been telling myself doesn't exist. The kind I don't know how to handle. The kind that makes me want to stop running and stay.

I shake my head, pushing the thoughts away, and head to my car.

I've got a Valentine's event to help set up. The irony still isn't lost on me.

As I drive toward the nursing home, my phone buzzes in the cupholder. Three new job alerts from Indeed. I've been applying to positions all week— marketing coordinator in Dallas, social media manager in Austin, content strategist in Houston, a few long-shot corporate communications roles that probably won't even respond.

Anything to prove to myself that I'm still planning to leave. Still moving forward. Still not staying in Ashen Mills permanently just because a certain cop makes me feel things I'm not ready to name.

I don't open the emails. Not yet. Can't handle more rejection notifications right now.

One crisis at a time, Gabby. One crisis at a time.

~

I balance two bins of decorations against my hip, pushing through the sliding doors of Ashen Mills Care Center while Mom calls out orders like a general preparing for battle.

"Streamers on the far wall, Gabby! Gift bags on the tables—make sure each one has candy and a card! Rhett, you can help hang the banner over the piano!"

"On it," he says somewhere behind me, voice even and easy like yesterday didn't happen. Like we didn't kiss in his kitchen. Like I didn't run away and ruin everything.

I don't turn around. Can't. Not yet.

I set the bins down on a folding table with more force than necessary, dust my hands off, and glance around the room.

Volunteers bustle between tables, unfolding paper hearts and sorting boxes of cookies—some of which Rhett and I made yesterday before I lost my mind and kissed him.

It should feel comforting—busy, purposeful, the good kind of chaos that comes from helping people. But all I can think about is the man on the ladder at the far side of the room, tacking up a red banner that reads *You Are Loved* in flowing script.

His sleeves are rolled to his elbows because of course they are, the muscles in his forearms flexing as he smooths out the wrinkles in the paper. He laughs at something Mrs. Patterson says from her wheelchair below, and she giggles like she's seventeen again, touching her pearls and blushing.

He has that effect on people. Makes them feel seen. Makes them feel like they matter.

Makes me feel like maybe I'm not as broken as I think I am.

I sigh and turn back to my boxes, unwrapping foam hearts and glittery garlands with probably more aggression than necessary. Anything to keep my hands busy and my brain distracted and my eyes from drifting back across the room to where he's being perfect without even trying.

"Sweetheart, can you grab the tape from Rhett?" Mom calls across the room, and I swear I see her smirk when I shoot her a look.

Of course. Because God must think this is hilarious.

"Sure," I say, forcing my voice into something neutral and normal. I make the walk slower than necessary, pretending to study the decorations we spent all afternoon hanging, buying time to get my face under control.

He notices me halfway there. His easy grin

softens into something quieter, more careful. Something flickering in his eyes I can't quite name but feel in my bones.

"Hey," he says when I reach him, quiet but warm.

"Hey." I can barely look at him. My eyes find a spot just past his shoulder, safer territory.

I hold out my hand. "Tape."

He hands it over without hesitation, letting our fingers brush for just a second longer than necessary. Just enough to make my pulse skip and my breath catch and every nerve ending in my body remember exactly what it felt like when those hands were on my waist, in my hair, pulling me closer like he'd been waiting his whole life for permission.

"Thanks," I say quickly, already turning away before I do something stupid like apologize or cry or ask him to kiss me again.

"Anytime."

The word follows me back across the room like a promise.

I tape hearts to the window with shaking hands, hyperaware of his presence even when I'm not looking. Every few minutes, I glance up—I can't help it —and every time, I catch him looking back. Not in a way that feels heavy or demanding or like he's waiting for an explanation.

Just... seeing me.

And I hate how much I like being seen.

RHETT

By the time the sun starts dipping low outside the nursing home windows, casting everything in that golden late-afternoon light, I'm pretty sure I've spent the entire day pretending not to watch her.

Which is exhausting.

She moves through the room like a quiet storm —focused, determined, just a little messy around the edges in a way that makes her more real than anyone I've ever known. Every time I think I've got my head back on straight, she laughs at something one of the residents says, or tucks a strand of hair behind her ear, or flashes that stubborn little smile when she's trying not to show she's proud of making someone happy.

And I'm done for all over again.

Completely, hopelessly done for.

There's no use denying it anymore. Somewhere between pulling her over on Highway 77 and kissing her in my flour-covered kitchen, I started falling for Gabby Wallace.

Hard.

The kind of falling that doesn't come with a

safety net or a guarantee or any promise that she'll catch me too.

Lord, I pray silently, adjusting a streamer that doesn't need adjusting. *I thought yesterday was good —I thought maybe she felt it too. But she's running again, and I don't know how to reach her without pushing her further away.*

Mrs. Rodriguez asks me to move a chair, and I do, grateful for something useful to do with my hands.

Help me be patient, I continue, my prayer becoming as natural as breathing. *Help me love her well even if that means loving her from a distance. Even if she never lets me close again.*

She's across the room now, helping one of the volunteers hang pink streamers. The light catches in her hair, turning brown into gold, and I swear I could stand here all day watching her and not regret a single second of it.

She's hurting, Lord. I can see it in the way she pulls back every time we get close. In the way she won't let herself be happy. In the way she looks at me sometimes like she wants to stay but doesn't know how.

I move to help Mr. Chen with his walker, steadying him as he makes his way to a chair.

Whatever she needs—whether that's space or time or just a friend who doesn't run when things get hard— help me be that. Help me see what she needs instead of just wanting what I want.

The balloon arch we spent an hour constructing chooses that exact moment to give up on life.

It happens fast—a sharp *pop* followed by a slow, tragic sagging of pink and white latex like a deflating dream. A few balloons roll away across the floor like escapees making a break for freedom.

"Seriously?" Gabby groans, hands on her hips, staring at the disaster with an expression that's half frustration, half resignation.

I can't help but smile as I head over. "Looks like our structural engineer failed us."

She shoots me a look that could melt steel. "Oh, don't start."

"I'm just saying, I warned you about the double-stick tape."

"And I told you it would hold."

"Technically..." I grin, gesturing at the sagging mess. "It didn't."

She narrows her eyes dangerously. "Technically, you're not helping."

"Guess that makes us both right."

Despite everything—despite the tension and the uncertainty and the way she's been avoiding my eyes all day—her mouth twitches. Almost a smile. Close enough that I count it as a win.

We fall into an easy rhythm after that, neither of us willing to admit we're enjoying this way too much. She holds the arch while I restring it, handing me pieces of twine like we're defusing a bomb instead of fixing party decorations. Every time our fingers brush, she pretends it doesn't send electricity up her arm.

I pretend I'm not counting how many times it happens.

Seven. It happens seven times, and each one feels like a gift.

By the time we finish, somehow everyone else has disappeared. The residents have been taken back to their rooms for dinner. The volunteers have packed up and gone home, promising to be back tomorrow for the actual event. Even Christie has vanished—probably on purpose, because she's not subtle at all about her matchmaking attempts.

It's just us in this big, quiet hall, surrounded by hearts and streamers and everything Gabby came here to avoid.

She sits cross-legged on the floor, sorting left-over paper hearts into piles—big, medium, small. Completely unnecessary organizing, but her hands always need something to do when she's thinking too hard.

"If I see another pink anything, I might actually revolt," she mutters, not looking up.

I sit beside her, stretching my legs out, close enough to feel the warmth radiating from her. "I'll call the chief, let him know there's a potential holiday-related crime in progress."

She snorts despite herself, shaking her head. "You think you're funny."

"I think *you* think I'm funny."

She looks at me then, finally looks at me, eyes meeting mine across the sea of paper hearts scattered between us. The fluorescent lights hum overhead. The old building settles and creaks. The world narrows to just the space between us.

"Why do you always do that?" she asks softly, voice barely above a whisper.

"Do what?"

"Make everything easy. Make me feel like..." She trails off, looking away.

"Like what?"

"Like maybe I'm not broken."

My chest tightens. "Gabby, you're not broken."

"You don't know that." Her voice cracks slightly on the last word.

"Yeah," I say quietly, meaning it with everything in me. "I do."

Help her see herself the way You see her, I pray silently. *The way I see her. Not broken. Not a failure. Just... her. Beautiful and stubborn and worth every bit of patience and time and love it takes.*

She looks away, blinking fast, and I can see her building those walls again brick by brick. "We should finish up. It's getting late."

I push to my feet, brushing off my jeans. "You always run when it gets serious."

"Do not."

"You do." I step closer, close enough to see the gold flecks in her eyes. "Every time."

She freezes. The air between us hums, heavy and familiar and terrifying.

"Maybe I have good reasons," she whispers.

"Maybe," I allow. "Or maybe you're just scared."

"Of what?"

"Of this." I gesture between us. "Of letting someone in who won't leave."

We work in silence for the next few minutes, finishing the cleanup. When the last trash bag's tied and the tables are straight and there's nothing left to busy ourselves with, I grab her tote bag before she can protest.

"I'll walk you out."

"You don't have to."

"I know."

Outside, the air's cold enough to see our breath, little clouds dissipating into the darkening sky. The parking lot's mostly empty, lamplight stretching long shadows across the asphalt. I set her bag on the hood of her car and lean against the fender.

She looks up at me, and I can see it written all over her face—the war between what she wants and what she's afraid of.

"Gabby," I say quietly, gently. "Why do you keep pulling back?"

Her lips part, but no words come. Then, to my

surprise—and maybe hers too—a single tear slips down her cheek, catching the lamplight.

I reach out before I can think better of it, brushing it away with my thumb, so gentle it makes my own chest ache. "Hey." My voice is softer now, careful. "It's okay."

She shakes her head, more tears threatening. "It's not you. I swear it's not you. It's just... me. I'm the problem. I always am."

"Then let me be here," I say, and I've never meant anything more in my life. "For you. With you. However you need me to be."

Her breath hitches, and for one dangerous, beautiful second, I think she might let me. Might actually let herself be vulnerable and real and trust that I won't run when she shows me the messy parts.

But then she steps back, the walls sliding into place so fast I can almost hear them lock.

"I should go."

"Gabby—"

"Big day tomorrow, right? The actual event?" Her voice is too bright, too forced. "I should get some sleep."

I don't argue. Don't push. Just nod even though I can see the disappointment in my own reflection in her eyes. "Yeah. Big day."

She unlocks her door, fumbles with her keys, anything to avoid looking at me.

"Gabby?"

She glances over, wary.

"Get home safe, alright?"

She swallows hard. "I will."

And then she's gone, taillights disappearing into the dark, leaving me standing there in the glow of the streetlamp with my hands in my pockets and my heart in my throat.

I don't know what else to do, Lord, I pray, watching until I can't see her car anymore. *I've been patient. I've given her space. I've tried to show her she's worth staying for.*

The February wind picks up, cold against my face.

But I can't force this. I can't make her trust me or choose me or believe that she deserves to be loved well.

I head to my truck, keys jingling in the quiet.

So I'm asking—help her see. Help her know. Help her believe that she's not too broken or too much or too anything. That she's exactly enough.

I start the engine, letting it warm up while I sit in the cold cab.

And if this isn't Your plan—if I'm supposed to let her go and just be her friend and nothing more—give me the strength to do that too. Because right now, Lord, I don't know how.

The prayer settles into my bones, familiar and steadying.

In Jesus' name, amen.

I put the truck in gear and drive home through the quiet streets of Ashen Mills, trying not to think about how empty my apartment is going to feel.

Trying not to wonder if she's thinking about me too.

Trying not to hope for something I'm not sure she can give.

But hoping anyway.

Because for all the ways she keeps pulling back, I can't shake the feeling that she's already halfway in my arms.

She just doesn't know it yet.

saturday, february 12th

GABBY

The red sundress wasn't my first choice. Or my second. Or even my fifth.

I tried on practically everything in my closet this morning—gray sweater, too depressing. Black dress, too funeral-ish. Jeans and a t-shirt, too casual for an event I helped plan. I even considered the floral thing I wore to my cousin's wedding last summer before realizing it still had a wine stain on the sleeve.

But after the week I've had—after the kiss and the running and the feelings I can't quite name—it felt wrong to show up in something safe and neutral.

So here I am, standing in front of the mirror in my childhood bedroom, tugging at the hem of this red sundress and trying to convince myself it's not too on theme. Not too Valentine's-y. Not too much like I'm trying.

Except I am trying. And I hate that I kind of like it.

The color makes my skin glow in a way I'd forgotten it could. Makes my eyes look brighter, less tired. Makes me look like someone who didn't spend last night replaying a kiss on an endless loop while stress-eating the cookies we made right before said kiss.

I add simple gold earrings, swipe on mascara, and call it done. Good enough for an event at a nursing home. Good enough to face him after everything.

When I pull into the parking lot at Ashen Mills Care Center, the place looks just as we left it yesterday. Paper hearts line the walkway, fluttering slightly in the February breeze. The banner Rhett and I wrestled with yesterday hangs proudly above the main entrance, slightly crooked but somehow perfect in its imperfection.

The scent of sugar cookies drifts through the cold air, sweet and inviting, mixing with the smell of fresh coffee someone's brewing inside.

Cars are already filling the lot—volunteers arriving early, family members bringing residents who live off-site, even a few people from town who just want to help. This event is bigger than I realized. Clearly this is really important.

And I helped make it happen.

The thought sits strange in my chest—pride mixed with something softer. Something that feels dangerously like belonging.

Inside, the event room hums with purposeful movement. Volunteers laugh as they arrange tables with red plastic tablecloths. Mom stands at the center with her ever-present clipboard, orchestrating everything like a maestro conducting a symphony— directing traffic, answering questions, somehow keeping track of forty different details at once.

She spots me and waves, her whole face lighting up. "Oh, good, you're here! We're almost ready to let the residents in. Can you believe it? We actually pulled this off!"

"I see that," I say, taking in the finished setup— the cards residents will decorate, the photo booth corner with heart-shaped props, the refreshment table groaning under the weight of cookies and punch. "It looks amazing, Mom. Really."

She smiles, pride softening her features, making her eyes shine. "We had good help this year. Really good help."

My eyes betray me, glancing across the room to where Rhett's helping an elderly man adjust decorative hearts on his walker. He's not in his uniform today—dark jeans that fit perfectly, white button-down with the sleeves already rolled to his forearms because of course they are—but somehow he still looks official.

And entirely too handsome for a man who gives traffic safety lectures for a living.

As if sensing my gaze, he looks up. Our eyes meet across the crowded room, and he smiles—small, genuine, a little uncertain.

My heart does that stupid flipping thing it's been doing all week.

I look away first, pretending to study the tablecloths.

"Alright, everyone!" Mom calls, clapping her hands once for attention. The room settles immediately, conversations tapering off. "Before we open the doors and let our wonderful residents in, I'd like to say something."

She looks around the room, her smile fond and a little teary in that way she gets when she's emotional but trying to hold it together. "Every year, Hearts and Hands reminds me why this community is so special. Why Ashen Mills feels like family. We don't have to do grand things to make a difference in someone's life. Sometimes it's as simple as a card with a kind word. A cookie made with love. A moment of attention that says 'you matter.'"

Her voice catches slightly. "That's love in action. That's what we're doing today."

A few people nod, murmuring agreement. Someone says "amen" softly.

Mom pauses, then gestures toward Rhett with her clipboard. "And this year, our very own Officer Lawson has expressed that he'd like to lead us in prayer before we begin. Rhett?"

Every head in the room turns toward him.

He clears his throat, rubbing the back of his neck in that self-conscious way he does when he's trying to hide how much something means to him. "Uh— thanks, Mrs. Wallace. I appreciate that."

Then he steps forward. Even the volunteers who were still fussing with decorations stop and turn.

"Let's pray."

The room quiets instantly. The only sounds are the faint hum of the heater, the rustle of paper hearts in the air conditioning, someone's phone vibrating in a pocket before being quickly silenced.

"God," he begins, and something in my chest tightens at the easy familiarity in his tone. Like he talks to God the same way he talks to everyone else —honest, direct, no pretense. "Thank You for this day. For the people in this room who gave their time and energy to make this happen. For the residents we're about to celebrate. For the chance to show love—not the kind that fades when the flowers die and the candy's gone, but the kind that lasts. The kind You teach us to give freely, without expecting anything back."

Someone sniffles. Mrs. Rodriguez, I think.

"Thank You for laughter," Rhett continues, "for second chances, for reminding us that love isn't just something we feel in our hearts—it's something we do with our hands. Help us to be patient today. Help us to be kind. Help us to make someone smile who maybe hasn't smiled in a while. Help us to see people the way You see them—as beloved, as worthy, as never forgotten."

He pauses, and in the silence I can hear my own heartbeat.

"In Jesus' name, amen."

A quiet murmur of "amen" ripples through the room like a wave, voices overlapping in agreement.

I've been to a lot of church events in my life. Youth group meetings and Sunday services and Easter sunrise celebrations where everyone's still half asleep. I've heard a lot of prayers—polished and practiced, carefully worded to sound impressive.

But this one does something I can't quite explain.

It feels like warmth spreading through my ribs. Like light reaching a corner I'd forgotten existed.

I look at him again—this man who somehow made it impossible to stay cynical, who paid my ticket without telling me, who kisses like he means it and prays like he believes it—and my heart just... overflows.

Not with fear this time.

With something else. Something bigger.

~

The residents are out in full force now—wheel-chairs parked strategically near tables, walkers lined carefully along the wall, and more smiles than I've seen in months. Decades, maybe.

There's pink punch in plastic cups and cookies on paper plates. The smell of sugar and vanilla floats through the air, mixing with the faint scent of the residents' perfume and aftershave. An endless loop of old love songs plays from speakers someone set up in the corner—Frank Sinatra, Etta James, Dean Martin crooning about romance and dancing and forever.

Mom's beaming near the refreshments, chatting animatedly with volunteers and residents alike. Rhett's across the room helping one of the residents fix a boutonniere that keeps sliding off his lapel.

Every few minutes, our eyes meet across the chaos. And every single time they do, my stomach flips like I'm sixteen again and just got asked to prom by the cute boy from math class.

Except this isn't high school. And Rhett Lawson is so much more than cute.

When the DJ announces that the dance floor is officially open, a cheer goes up from the residents.

And then Mr. Harold Mason, age eighty-four and

notorious flirt, hobbles toward me with his polished wooden cane.

"Well now, Miss Wallace," he says, offering his hand with old-fashioned gallantry. "Would you do an old man the honor of a dance?"

I can't help smiling. "I'd be delighted, Mr. Mason."

He grins, revealing the gap where his left canine used to be. "Call me Harold, sweetheart. Mr. Mason makes me feel ancient."

"You *are* ancient," I tease gently.

"Fair point." He leads me toward the center of the makeshift dance floor, moving carefully but with surprising grace. "But I've still got some moves left."

We sway to the music—some slow song about moonlight and romance that I vaguely recognize from my grandparents' record collection. Around us, other couples join in. Volunteers dancing with residents. Family members with their elderly parents. Even Mom gets pulled onto the floor by Mr. Chen, who apparently taught ballroom dancing in the '60s and hasn't forgotten a single step.

"You're good at this," I tell Harold as he guides me through a gentle turn.

"Don't sound so surprised, young lady," he says, chuckling. "I used to teach my wife to dance right here in this very hall. Back when it was the community center and we were both younger than you are now."

"She was a lucky woman."

His expression softens, eyes going distant with memory. "I was the lucky one. Sixty-two years we had together before the Lord called her home. Not a day I don't miss her."

My throat tightens. "I'm sorry."

"Don't be. I got sixty-two years of the best kind of love. That's more than most folks get." He glances over my shoulder, and a mischievous smile crosses his weathered face. "Speaking of which... he's watching you, you know."

I blink. "Who?"

He lifts a bushy white eyebrow. "That officer fella. The one who's been pretending to refill the punch bowl for the last ten minutes even though it's still half full."

I turn just enough to spot Rhett leaning against the refreshment table, red plastic cup in hand, eyes fixed directly on me. When our gazes meet, he doesn't look away. Just smiles slightly and raises his cup in a small salute.

The sight makes my pulse stutter.

Harold chuckles low. "Didn't mean to start trouble. But if I were a younger man—and a betting man—I'd put money on him being head over heels for you."

"He isn't...that's not..."

"Sweetheart, I've been around long enough to know a look when I see one. That's not just interest.

That's the real deal." He pats my hand with his papery-thin one. "Go on."

I laugh despite myself, shaking my head. "You're impossible, Harold."

"Maybe. But I'm right." The song ends, and he bows slightly—actually bows. "Thank you for the dance, Miss Wallace. Now go claim what's yours before someone else does."

"He's not mine to claim."

Harold just winks. "Yet."

Before I can talk myself out of it, before I can overthink or build walls or run away like I always do, I smooth my dress and cross the room.

Rhett straightens as I approach, surprise flickering across his face before settling into something warmer.

I stop in front of him, heart thudding so loud I'm sure he can hear it. "I believe," I say, holding out my hand with more confidence than I feel, "I owe you one more dance."

His smile is slow and genuine and absolutely devastating. "You do."

He sets down his cup and takes my hand, and I'm about to let him pull me toward the slower music when the opening beats of "Cupid Shuffle" suddenly blast through the speakers.

We both freeze. Then burst out laughing.

"Well," he says, grinning, "guess we better follow instructions."

"To the right, to the right," I sing under my breath as we join the growing crowd of residents, volunteers, staff, and even my mom, all shuffling in gloriously uneven lines.

Rhett's beside me, trying and completely failing to stay coordinated, bumping my shoulder every few steps and stepping on his own feet at least twice.

"You're terrible at this," I tell him, laughing so hard my sides hurt.

"Don't laugh," he warns, but he's grinning too wide for it to be serious.

"Oh, I'm *definitely* laughing."

"Traitor."

The room feels alive—wheelchairs spinning in rhythm, staff clapping along, laughter bouncing off the walls and ceiling like it's trying to escape. Rhett grabs my hand halfway through the chorus and spins me once, earning a cheer from the residents watching from the sidelines.

I'm laughing so hard I can barely breathe, barely see through the happy tears. The warmth of his hand wrapped around mine, our eyes catching and holding in the swirl of pink and gold and red decorations.

For the first time in years—maybe in my entire adult life—Valentine's Day doesn't feel like something I'm surviving.

It feels like something I'm living.

RHETT

I lean against the doorway for a second, just watching. Just taking it all in.

It's chaos in the best possible way—paper hearts dangling as the tape comes loose from the wall, pink punch spilling on the floor in small puddles, someone's walker tangled in streamers that need to be cut free—but somehow, it all works.

It's joy. Pure and unfiltered and real.

And at the center of it all is Gabby.

She's laughing with one of the nurses about something, her red dress bright and vibrant against the sea of pastels and whites. Her cheeks are flushed from dancing, her eyes lit up in a way I haven't seen before, and she's holding a tray of cookies like she was born to run events like this.

It hits me right then, standing in this doorway watching her be happy—how different she looks when she isn't running. When she isn't guarded or sarcastic or waiting for the next thing to go wrong. When she's just... here. Present. Alive. Herself.

And I swear, my chest physically hurts with how much I love seeing her like this.

Thank You, I pray silently. *For this. For her. For today.*

"Officer Lawson," a voice says beside me, snapping me out of it. It's Christie—Gabby's mom—smiling like she already knows exactly what I was thinking. "You've done such a wonderful job this week. The residents keep saying it's the best Hearts and Hands event we've had in years."

I rub the back of my neck, uncomfortable with the praise. "Wasn't me, ma'am. Your daughter deserves all the credit."

"She surprised herself," Christie says softly, following my gaze to where Gabby's now crouched beside a table, helping one of the older men check his bingo card with infinite patience. "She didn't think she could do something like this. Didn't think she belonged here."

"She was wrong."

"Yes, she was." Christie turns to look at me directly, her eyes knowing. "You have that effect on people, you know. You make them want to show up. Want to be better."

I don't know what to say to that, so I just smile and head over to help with the next round of bingo before I get too emotional about a woman in a red dress who makes my heart do impossible things.

~

By the time the last table's cleared and the banner's starting to sag again—we really should have used better tape—the nursing home feels quiet in that satisfied, tired way that follows good events.

Volunteers trickle out one by one, arms full of leftover cookies wrapped in foil and empty punch bowls that need washing. The residents wave from their doorways, still clutching their cards and prizes, still smiling, still radiating that particular kind of happiness that comes from being remembered.

Gabby stands by the entrance beside her mom, saying goodbye to a group of teenagers from the youth group who came to help. The red of her dress glows soft under the hallway lights, and even with glitter somehow in her hair and exhaustion written across her face, she's the most beautiful thing in this building.

In this town.

Maybe in the world.

"Hey," I say as I approach, my voice coming out softer than I intended. "You did good today."

She glances up at me, and a small, genuine smile breaks through the tiredness. "So did you."

Her mom turns just in time to catch us looking at each other. "I'm heading out, sweetheart," she tells Gabby.

Gabby nods quickly. "I'll see you at home."

I help her lift her bag from the floor and brush a

stray ribbon off the strap before handing it over. "Here you go."

"Thanks," she says, and for a second our eyes catch and hold. There's so much I want to say—*thank you, I'm sorry for pushing, please don't go, I think I'm falling for you*—but I just nod instead.

She turns toward the door, and I watch her go.

She pauses, looks back over her shoulder. "Night, Rhett."

My name in her voice. Simple. Soft. Everything.

~

No matter how many times I replay today—the prayer, the dancing, the way she looked at me during Cupid Shuffle—I can't stop thinking about her smile.

I've had enough of silence.

I grab my phone and scroll until I find her name. My thumb hovers over the call button for exactly three seconds before I press it.

It only takes one ring.

"Hey," she answers, soft and cautious. Maybe a little surprised.

"Hey yourself." I lean against the kitchen counter, rubbing the back of my neck. "Just wanted to make sure you made it home okay."

"I did. Thanks for checking."

There's a beat of quiet. Neither of us seems ready

to hang up, but neither of us knows exactly where to start or what to say next.

"You did good today," I say finally, because it's true and I want her to know it.

"You already told me that."

"I meant it both times."

She laughs quietly—just a breath of sound, but it's enough to make everything feel right again.

I close my eyes, letting the sound of her voice fill the empty spaces in my kitchen.

"Listen," I say, "you doing anything tomorrow after church?"

She hesitates. I can practically hear her thinking, weighing, building walls. "Why?"

"Thought maybe we could grab lunch. Or coffee. Something normal that doesn't involve glue sticks or glitter explosions."

Her silence stretches a little too long. A little too careful.

"Gabby?"

"This isn't a good idea, Rhett." Her voice is steady, but I can hear the door closing. The wall going up. The retreat beginning.

Frustration flares in my chest. "Why not?"

"Because." She sighs. "Because you're... you, and I'm me, and I just...I can't..."

"Gabby, stop," I cut in, sharper than I mean to. All the patience I've been practicing for two weeks suddenly evaporating. "You keep saying this like it's supposed to make sense, but it doesn't. Not to me. I don't get what you're so scared of."

"I'm not scared," she snaps back, defensive.

"Then prove it." The words come out rough, too frustrated to pull back now. "Stop running every time things start to feel real. Stop making excuses. Just... stop."

Silence. Just her quiet breathing on the other end of the line.

Then, softly, with an edge I've never heard before: "Really, Rhett? Excuses?"

The guilt hits instantly. "Gabby, I didn't mean—"

"I gotta go."

"Gabby, wait—"

The line clicks dead.

I drop my head back against the cabinet and let out a long, slow breath that does nothing to ease the tightness in my chest.

"Nice job, Lawson," I mutter to the empty kitchen. "Real smooth."

The phone feels heavy in my hand. The house doesn't smell like sugar cookies anymore.

It smells like regret.

sunday, february 13th

GABBY

The sunlight filters through the blinds in my childhood bedroom in long golden stripes, cutting across my comforter like little reminders that the world's still spinning even when I'd rather hit pause and hide under the covers forever.

Mom's already gone when I shuffle into the kitchen—her usual Sunday morning whirlwind of perfume and purpose, coffee made and dishes in the sink—and she's left a note on the counter in her looping handwriting.

See you at church, sweetheart.
Bring your smile.

I stare at it longer than I should, fingers tracing the curve of her words, because I'm not entirely sure I have a smile to bring today.

Rhett hasn't texted since last night.

Not that I expected him to. Not after the way our phone call ended—his voice sharp with frustration finally breaking through all that patience, mine clipped and defensive, both of us saying things we probably shouldn't have said, both of us meaning them anyway.

I've replayed that conversation more times than I'd admit to anyone. His words keep circling back: *Stop running every time things start to feel real.*

He wasn't wrong.

He never really is, and that might be what bothers me most.

I told myself I wasn't running. Told myself I was just being smart, protecting myself, keeping my heart safe from another inevitable disappointment. But sitting here now in this quiet kitchen, staring at my cold cup of coffee and Mom's cheerful note, the difference between protecting myself and running away feels a lot smaller than I want to admit.

Maybe there's no difference at all.

By the time I walk into Ashen Mills Baptist, the sanctuary smells exactly the way it always does— lemon polish and old hymnals and that particular scent of wood and faith that I've known my entire life. It smells like nostalgia. Like coming home whether I want to or not.

It's a smaller crowd today—Valentine's weekend means people are traveling, visiting family, or sleeping in—but there's still enough to fill the pews with the warm hum of conversation and community.

I spot Mom near the front, already deep in conversation with Mrs. Henderson about something event-related, and I slide into the seat beside her just as the organ begins its soft prelude. Sunlight spills through the stained-glass window above the pulpit, casting little splashes of pink and gold and blue across the worn carpet, making everything look softer somehow.

We sing a few hymns—voices rising in imperfect harmony, Mrs. Taylor's soprano soaring above everyone else's like it always does—and for a little while, it feels good to lose myself in the sound. To let the music fill all the spaces where thoughts about Rhett keep trying to take root.

But then the last chord fades, the congregation settles, and Pastor Miller steps to the pulpit with his well-worn Bible already open, his reading glasses sliding down his nose the way they always do.

"Church," he says, his voice warm as the wood in this room, familiar as Sunday morning itself, "our text today is from First John, chapter four, verses seven through twelve."

He reads it plain and steady, no dramatic flourishes, just the words themselves:

"Beloved, let us love one another, for love is from God, and whoever loves has been born of God and knows God. Anyone who does not love does not know God, because God is love. In this the love of God was made manifest among us, that God sent his only Son into the world, so that we might live through him. In this is love, not that we loved God but that he loved us and sent his Son to be the propitiation for our sins. Beloved, if God so loved us, we also ought to love one another."

The words feel ancient and somehow brand-new at the same time. Older than this building. Older than this town. But landing fresh in my chest like I'm hearing them for the first time.

Pastor Miller closes the Bible softly, both palms resting on the pulpit, and looks out at us with that gentle expression he gets when he's about to say something that matters.

"Now, I know what tomorrow is," he says, mouth quirking in a small smile. "There are pink aisles at the Dollar General to prove it. Heart-shaped everything. Chocolate. Flowers. Teddy bears holding signs about love."

A ripple of chuckles moves through the congregation. Someone behind me mutters "amen."

"But the love John's talking about here?" Pastor Miller continues, tapping the Bible. "It isn't chocolate-shaped. It isn't card-shaped. It isn't even romance-shaped, though romance can certainly be part of it."

He pauses, letting that sink in.

"The love John's talking about is Jesus-shaped."

The sanctuary goes quiet. Even the usual rustling of bulletins stops.

"See, our culture has this idea about love," he says, his voice getting that particular quality it gets when he's building toward something important. "The world tells us love is a feeling. A mood we fall into. Something that happens *to* us when we meet the right person or have the right experience. We fall in love, we say. Like it's gravity. Like we have no choice."

He shakes his head slowly.

"But that's not the love the Bible talks about. Not even close."

He leans forward slightly, like he's sharing a secret.

"Real love—the Jesus kind—isn't a mood we fall into. It's a cross-shaped choice we make. Every single day. It's Jesus washing His disciples' feet even when He knew one of them would betray Him before morning. It's Him feeding the crowds who would shout 'crucify Him' a week later. It's Him on that cross saying 'Father, forgive them' when forgiveness was the last thing they deserved."

My throat tightens.

"Love—real love—moves *toward* the mess," Pastor Miller says, his voice gentle but absolutely sure. "Not away from it. It doesn't wait for the other person to get their act together. It doesn't keep score. It doesn't say 'I'll love you when you're worthy' because the whole point is that none of us are worthy. That's why Jesus had to come."

Someone says "amen" quietly.

"This week, the world's gonna tell you that love is romance and roses and grand gestures," he continues. "And those things can be wonderful expressions of love. But they're not love itself. Love itself is showing up. It's serving quietly when no one's watching. It's calling someone by name and actually seeing them. It's writing a note that says 'we haven't forgotten you' to someone who thought everyone had."

My shoulders have been tense since he started talking, waiting for the part where he tells us romantic love is frivolous or wrong or less important than other kinds of love. But that's not what he's saying at all.

He's saying it's *different.*

And I can breathe again.

"If we wait until we *feel* loving," Pastor Miller says, and this is the part I can tell he really wants us to hear because his voice drops lower, more intimate, "we will love almost no one. Because feelings are fickle. They change with the weather and our hormones and whether we got enough sleep last night."

A few people laugh.

"But the Jesus kind of love?" He taps the Bible again. "It acts first. It chooses first. And the feelings? They catch up later."

That lands in my chest like a stone dropping into still water, ripples spreading out to places I didn't know were empty.

It acts first. Feelings catch up later.

"So here's what I want to leave you with," Pastor Miller says, lifting three fingers. "Three small practices for living out this big command to love one another:

"One—*see people*. Call them by name. Look up from your phone, your hurry, your own problems long enough to notice the human being in front of you. God sees you. He calls you by name. Do the same for others.

"Two—*serve quietly*. No spotlight needed. No credit required. Just do the thing that needs doing because love is a verb, not a noun. Love acts.

"And three—*speak life*. You have no idea—*no idea*—how much power your words have. Proverbs says 'anxiety weighs down the heart, but a kind word cheers it up.' Church, we get to be those words. We get to be the oxygen someone else needs to breathe today."

He closes his Bible gently, both hands resting on it like it's precious.

"Jesus didn't love us because we deserved it. He loved us because He *is* love. And He's asking us to do the same—to love the difficult people, the messy people, the people who hurt us, the people we don't understand. To move toward them instead of away."

My mom hums an agreement beside me, already fishing in her purse for a pen so she can write that Proverbs quote in the margin of her bulletin. She'll probably have it framed and hanging in the fellowship hall by Wednesday, right next to the coffee maker.

But I just sit there, completely still, feeling something unravel in my chest. Something that's been knotted tight for weeks. Maybe months. Maybe years.

By the time Pastor Miller bows his head to lead us in prayer, my throat is so tight I can barely swallow.

Real love acts first. Feelings catch up later.

The words loop in my mind, soft but relentless, like they're burrowing down into places I've kept locked.

I think about Rhett.

His easy laugh that makes everyone around him lighter. The way he always shows up—to the church event, to help me with supplies, to my parents' house for dinner, to rescue me from Mrs. Carmichael's grocery store dramatics. The steadiness in his voice when he prayed yesterday over a room full of people, asking God to help us see each other the way He sees us.

The way he looks at people like he actually sees them. Like he's choosing to.

He's been doing it since the moment he pulled me over on Highway 77.

Choosing to see me.

To be kind even when I made it difficult.

To stay patient even when I gave him every reason not to be.

To show up over and over and over again, asking for nothing in return except maybe a dance or a shared meal or a moment of my time.

And what have I done?

Bolted.

Made jokes to deflect every time things got too real.

Protected myself from something that doesn't even look like the kind of love that's hurt me before.

Because this? What Rhett's been showing me?

This is different.

It's not perfect—he lost his patience last night, said things that stung. But it's *patient*. It's steady. It's the kind of love that acts first and hopes the feelings catch up.

It's cross-shaped.

And maybe—maybe—that's exactly what I've been too scared to believe could be real.

Too scared to trust.

Too scared to let myself receive.

Pastor Miller's voice softens for the final prayer. "Lord, teach us to love like You love. To see people the way You see them. To move toward the mess instead of away from it. To choose love even when— *especially* when—it's hard. Amen."

The congregation echoes it, a quiet chorus of amens that feels heavier than usual. More weighted with meaning.

When the service ends, everyone stands, chatting and hugging in the aisles like they always do. Mom's immediately pulled into conversation with someone from the music team about next week's special song. I slip out into the sunlight before she can catch me, before anyone can ask if I'm okay, because I'm not sure I could answer honestly.

Outside, the February air is crisp and clean, the parking lot glinting with puddles from last night's rain catching the late morning sun. I cross my arms, hugging myself against the chill that has nothing to do with the temperature.

Rhett's truck isn't here.

I scan the parking lot twice, just to be sure, but his familiar dark blue pickup is nowhere to be seen.

I tell myself I don't care. That it's fine. That

maybe a little space will help us both cool down after last night.

But the truth hits harder than I expect, settling heavy in my stomach.

I notice he's not here.

I miss him.

And it hurts.

Because I'm not sure anymore if I've been running to protect myself—or just running from something real because real things can hurt you and I've had enough hurt to last a lifetime.

But real things can also save you.

And maybe I've been so busy protecting my heart from pain that I never gave it a chance to heal.

I take a deep breath, the sermon still echoing in my head like a song I can't shake.

Love moves toward the mess, not away from it.

It acts first. Feelings catch up later.

I've been waiting to feel safe enough to love someone.

But maybe that's backwards.

Maybe you choose to love, and safety comes from the choosing.

I pull out my phone, thumb hovering over Rhett's name, but I can't quite make myself press it.

Tomorrow.

Tomorrow is Valentine's Day.

And for the first time since I drove back into this

town with my tail between my legs and a plan to hide from romance forever, I don't want to skip it.

I want to show up.

I want to choose.

I want to be brave enough to move toward love instead of away.

RHETT

Some Sundays remind you why you left the city.

Some remind you why you chose a small town.

And some—like today—remind you that being a cop means you show up for the hard things no matter if you are in the city or a small town.

The highway outside Ashen Mills is slick from last night's rain, water still pooling in the low spots where the drainage isn't great. A pickup lost traction on a curve about two miles out, clipped the guardrail hard enough to leave paint, and spun sideways into the median.

When I got the call, I was halfway through my second cup of coffee and halfway to church, already running late because I couldn't sleep last night, kept replaying that phone call with Gabby on a loop until three in the morning.

By the time I pull my truck in behind the ambulance, the world's gone gray—low clouds threatening more rain, the smell of fuel and wet asphalt and hot rubber hanging heavy in the cold air.

The driver's shaken but okay. Airbag deployed, seatbelt did its job. We get him checked out, stabilized, calm down the woman in the SUV who called it in and keeps apologizing like it's somehow her fault. I direct traffic around the scene while the tow truck hooks up, make sure nobody else slides out in the slick conditions.

It's nothing like the wrecks I used to work back in Houston—but it still gets under my skin the way these things always do.

When it's finally over and the scene's clear, I just sit on my truck for a minute, engine humming, radio crackling with the usual small-town Sunday chatter. I rub the back of my neck, trying to shake off the heaviness that clings to calls like this, and check my watch.

11:45 AM.

Church ended fifteen minutes ago.

I lean my head back against the seat and close my eyes.

Lord, I know You've got bigger things to worry about than me missing a sermon. But I could've used one today.

My phone sits silent in my pocket. No messages. No missed calls.

Nothing from Gabby.

Not that I expected anything after last night. I was too harsh. Pushed too hard. Said things I meant but probably shouldn't have said that way.

My stomach growls, pulling me out of my thoughts. I haven't eaten since yesterday, and the adrenaline from the accident scene is wearing off, leaving me shaky and tired.

I swing by the grocery store on the edge of town —the one that still plays old country music through ceiling speakers that buzz like a hive of confused bees. The parking lot's nearly empty on a Sunday afternoon, just a few cars scattered across the asphalt.

Inside, I grab a basket and head for the deli section. Rotisserie chicken. Loaf of bread. Some of those deli pickles that come in the big jar. A bottle of sweet tea because I'm too tired to make my own. Basic. Practical. Enough to get me through the next few days without having to think too hard about cooking.

I'm heading toward the registers when I pass the seasonal aisle.

And stop dead in my tracks.

Pink. Everywhere.

Stuffed bears in every size holding hearts that say things like "I Love You Beary Much" and "You're

Paws-itively Perfect." Plastic roses in shades of red and pink that no actual rose has ever been. Rows and rows of candy boxes shaped like hearts, shaped like lips, shaped like cupid's arrows. Balloons. Cards. Decorative pillows. Throw blankets. Candles that smell like "Romance" and "Passion" and probably just sugar and artificial fragrance.

It's aggressively, unapologetically Valentine's Day.

And standing here looking at it, Gabby's voice plays in my head clear as day.

I came back here to skip Valentine's Day. No romance, no roses, no pressure.

That was her plan. Hide out. Avoid the holiday. Pretend it doesn't exist.

And last night on the phone, I pushed her. Got frustrated. Told her to stop running.

But standing here in the middle of the world's tackiest pink battlefield, something settles in my chest like certainty.

There's no chance, absolutely zero chance, I'm letting her skip Valentine's Day.

Not without a fight.

Not when I know she deserves to be celebrated, to be chosen, to be loved well even when she doesn't think she does.

I grab a cart.

A bouquet of red roses? Let's make it two dozen. The biggest, most obnoxious bouquet they have.

Heart-shaped box of chocolates? Absolutely. The fancy kind with the little map inside showing what each piece is.

A bag of those chalky conversation hearts that taste like sweetened regret but are quintessentially Valentine's Day? Perfect. Three bags.

A card with a cheesy joke about love and law enforcement that makes me groan even as I grab it? Goes in the cart.

Pink tissue paper. Red ribbon. A small stuffed bear because why not. Another box of chocolates because you can never have too much chocolate.

And just for good measure—one single pink balloon shaped like a heart, because subtlety has clearly left the building.

A kid maybe ten years old stops in the middle of the aisle, staring at my overflowing cart with wide eyes. "Whoa. That's a lot of Valentine's stuff, mister."

I grin at him. "Don't judge, son. This is official police business."

His mom laughs, pulling him along. "Good luck with that."

"Thanks. I'm gonna need it."

By the time I reach the register, my cart looks like Cupid personally threw up in it. The cashier— teenage girl with pink streaks in her hair raises her eyebrows.

"Big Valentine's plans?" she asks, starting to scan items.

"Something like that."

"Must be some girl."

"Yeah." I swipe my card, watching the total climb. "She is."

Because the thing is, Gabby Wallace *is* some girl. She's funny and stubborn and scared and brave all at once. She shows up even when she doesn't want to. She makes me laugh. She makes me think. She makes me want to be the kind of man worth staying for.

And tomorrow, Valentine's Day, she's not hiding.

Not if I have anything to say about it.

I load everything into my truck, the bags crinkling and rustling, the balloon bobbing against the ceiling.

My phone still shows no messages.

But that's okay.

Because sure, today was rough. The accident. Missing church. The silence between us.

But tomorrow?

Tomorrow, I'm showing up.

Tomorrow, I'm choosing to love first and pray the feelings catch up.

Tomorrow, Gabby Wallace is getting the Valentine's Day she tried to skip.

Whether she's ready or not.

monday, february 14th

GABBY

My alarm goes off at seven.

By seven-oh-two, my heart is racing with a combination of terror and determination that I'm choosing to call bravery.

The sunlight spilling through my curtains feels too bright, too cheerful, too *Valentine's-y* for how knotted my stomach is. But I throw the covers back anyway, drag myself out of bed, and pull on the first semi-clean pair of jeans I find.

There's no real plan—just this restless, relentless tug in my chest that won't quit. The same feeling that's been building since Pastor Miller's sermon yesterday, since I realized I've been running from exactly what I've been looking for all along.

Love that acts first.

Love that chooses.

Love that moves toward the mess instead of away from it.

And Rhett Lawson? He's been doing that since the moment he pulled me over on Highway 77 two weeks ago.

Two weeks.

It sounds crazy. Impossible. Like something out of a movie where the timeline doesn't matter because it's fiction.

But this isn't fiction. This is real.

By the time I make it to the grocery store, it's barely eight AM and the parking lot's half empty, just a few early birds and people who apparently also forgot Valentine's Day existed until this morning. The automatic doors whoosh open, and I head straight for the Valentine's aisle with purpose.

Except it looks like it's survived an apocalypse.

Shredded gift wrap littering the floor. Broken candy hearts scattered across the shelves. Cards picked over until only the weird ones are left—the ones with jokes that don't quite land or sentiments that are trying way too hard. And exactly one bouquet of roses sitting in a bucket, looking like it's seen significantly better days.

I stand there in the wreckage, hands on my hips, scanning what's left.

What do you even get a man like Rhett Lawson?

He's the kind of guy who would actually appreciate a heartfelt card—probably frame it and put it on his refrigerator like it's art. But that feels too serious, too much pressure for someone who's known him for fourteen days. Chocolate? Too predictable. Flowers? He's a *guy*, and while I'm sure he'd appreciate them, it feels backwards.

Then I see it.

Slumped against the far wall like it's given up on life, one ear permanently bent at an odd angle, its tag barely hanging on by a thread—the giant, ridiculous teddy bear.

Similar to the one Rhett tried to buy during our chaotic Dollar General shopping trip. The one he looked genuinely sad to put back on the shelf.

A laugh bubbles up before I can stop it. "This'll do," I mutter, grabbing it by its floppy arm.

The cashier gives me a sympathetic look when she rings it up. "For your Valentine, huh?"

"Something like that."

"Must be someone special to deserve that bear at eight in the morning."

I swipe my card, refusing to calculate the damage to my already-pathetic bank account. "Yeah. He really is."

Then I lug the bear to my car—because it's genuinely massive and awkward and keeps flopping over—wrestle it into the passenger seat, and buckle the seatbelt across its middle because honestly, it feels like the right thing to do. Safety first, even for stuffed animals.

"Don't look at me like that," I grumble at it as I start the engine, my hands shaking slightly on the steering wheel. "We're doing something brave, okay? Something completely terrifying and possibly stupid and definitely not in the original plan."

The bear says nothing, just stares ahead with its glassy eyes.

I pull out of the parking lot and head toward Main Street, my heart thudding so loud it might as well have its own siren. Every turn feels too fast and too slow at the same time. Every red light an eternity.

What am I doing? He probably doesn't even want to see me. After I hung up on him. After I've spent two weeks pushing him away every time he got close.

But then Pastor Miller's voice echoes in my head. *Love acts first. Feelings catch up later.*

So I'm acting.

And praying desperately that my feelings aren't the only ones doing the catching up.

Ten minutes later—though it feels like both seconds and hours—my tires squeal slightly as I turn onto Main Street.

His truck's in the parking lot of the hardware store.

Good. He's home.

No turning back now.

I park on the street, unbuckle the bear, and somehow manage to haul it up the stairs without dropping it or losing my nerve entirely. The "Welcome to the Love Shack" mat mocks me with its cheerfulness.

I knock.

Nothing.

I knock again, louder this time, my knuckles rapping against the wood with more confidence than I actually feel.

Still nothing.

Please be home. Please don't make me stand out here holding a giant teddy bear like a crazy person.

Finally, the door creaks open, and Rhett stands there looking like every romance novel cover I've ever pretended not to read.

Barefoot. Hair messy from sleep, sticking up in about five different directions. Eyes squinting like the February sunlight personally attacked him. Wearing a soft gray T-shirt that's just fitted enough to show his shoulders and joggers that should absolutely be illegal in at least three states.

He looks confused and sleepy and so stupidly, devastatingly handsome that I momentarily forget why I'm here.

"Gabby?" His voice is scratchy, low, rough with sleep. "It's... eight in the morning."

"I know." The words tumble out faster than my

brain can organize them, tripping over each other in their hurry to escape. "I know it's early and you're probably still sleepy and I should've texted first but I didn't know what to say and I was afraid if I waited I'd chicken out so I just...I'm here. I'm here and I don't want to skip Valentine's Day anymore."

He blinks at me, processing. "What?"

I take a breath, steadying myself. "This," I say, shoving the bear at him with more force than necessary, nearly knocking him backwards. "This is for you. I got you a Valentine. Because I'm done running. I'm done pretending I..." I gesture helplessly between us. "I'm just ready, okay?"

He looks from me to the bear and then back to me again.

And his lips twitch.

Then curve.

Then break into the most genuine, beautiful smile I've ever seen on a human face.

"Well," he says slowly, voice still rough but warmer now, "about time."

"Just take the stupid thing, Rhett."

He takes it, tucking it under one arm like it weighs nothing, and his eyes—those impossibly warm brown eyes—find mine and hold.

"Are you asking me to be your Valentine, Gabby Wallace?"

My breath catches. "I—maybe? Yes. I don't know. Is that what this is?"

"That's exactly what this is." His smile softens into something that makes my knees weak. "And for the record? Best Valentine's invitation I've ever gotten."

RHETT

She's standing on my porch at eight in the morning on Valentine's Day, hair messy like she didn't brush it, cheeks pink from the cold or embarrassment or both.

And I'm pretty sure I've never loved anything more in my entire life.

"You better come in," I say, shifting the bear under one arm and nudging the screen door open wider with my foot. "Before the town starts forming their own theories."

She hesitates for just a second, glancing down at her sneakers like she's debating whether this is a terrible idea or just mildly catastrophic. Then, with a resigned sigh that somehow sounds hopeful, she follows me inside.

The second she steps through the doorway, I remember exactly how small my apartment is—and how much of a mess I made in my Valentine's preparation frenzy yesterday.

She stops dead in the middle of my living room, taking in the scene.

Two dozen roses crammed into a glass vase that's definitely too small, leaning precariously against each other beside a heart-shaped box of chocolates. Three different bags of conversation hearts scattered across the counter like confetti, some of them already opened because I got hungry waiting and stress-ate half a bag. The card with a handwritten note that took me over an hour to write. And a red heart balloon bobbing gently above it all.

Her head tilts slowly as she processes the chaos. "What... is all this?"

I scratch the back of my neck, suddenly feeling like a middle-schooler who got caught trying way too hard to impress his crush. "This," I say, gesturing vaguely at the Valentine's explosion that is currently my living room, "was supposed to be your morning surprise."

Her eyebrow arches, unimpressed. "You were going to surprise me?"

"Yeah." I lean a hip against the counter, trying for casual and missing by approximately a mile. "I was gonna let you sleep in—you know, until a reasonable hour, since it's Valentine's Day and all—

then show up at your parents' house with all this and ask you to be my Valentine."

"With all this?" She gestures at the chaos. "You were going to bring all of this to my house?"

"Well, yeah."

She stares at me for a long moment, and I can't tell if she's about to laugh or cry or tell me I'm completely insane.

Then her expression softens. "You bought me two dozen roses."

"I did."

"And a card?"

"Yep."

Her lips twitch. "This is...a lot."

"Maybe." I step closer, my voice dropping lower. "But I wasn't about to let you spend another Valentine's Day alone, Gabby. Or skip it just because you think it's easier that way."

Her eyes flick up to mine, searching for something. The smart comeback on her tongue never comes.

I take another step, closing the distance between us. "You came speeding back into this town two weeks ago like you were trying to outrun the whole world."

She lets out a short laugh, shaking her head. "You make it sound so dramatic. I just got fired and needed a place to stay."

"Maybe. But the second I saw you pulled over on

that shoulder—I knew there was more to it than just a job loss."

Her gaze flickers, curious now, guarded but listening. "More to what?"

"More to you." Another step. We're close enough now that I can see the exact moment her breath catches. "You've got that look—like you're pretending not to care because caring has hurt you too many times. Like you're convinced that if you don't let anyone close, you can't be disappointed when they leave."

She swallows hard, and I watch her throat work. The air between us shifts, gets heavier.

"And I get it," I say quietly, gently, because this is the important part and I need her to really hear it. "People leave. Things fall apart. Jobs end and relationships fail and sometimes the people who are supposed to stay don't. But Gabby—some things, some people—they're worth staying for. Worth fighting for. Worth showing up for even when it's scary."

She looks up at me, all that guarded humor and vulnerability warring in her hazel eyes. "You're very dramatic, you know that?"

"Maybe." I grin. "But I'm also right."

She shakes her head, but that smile she keeps trying to fight finally breaks through, lighting up her whole face.

I step even closer, my voice quieter this time,

more serious. "You know, I had this whole plan. Was gonna knock on your door around nine, hand you some cheesy card and those roses, maybe convince you to let me take you to breakfast. And then, if you didn't slam the door in my face, I was gonna ask if you'd dance with me in your kitchen."

Her lips twitch. "Dance in my kitchen?"

"Still owe me that third dance, remember? And I figured if you were gonna finally give it to me, might as well make it count."

"I did give you that third dance." She protests.

"Gabby, the Cupid Shuffle does not count."

She's quiet for a moment, just looking at me. Then, so softly I almost miss it. "You really weren't going to let me skip today."

"Not a chance," I say honestly. "You deserve to be celebrated, Gabby. You deserve someone who shows up and doesn't give up and thinks you're worth two dozen wilted roses and terribly cheesy cards and whatever else it takes."

A tear slips down her cheek. "I don't know how to do this. How to let someone—"

"Then let me show you." I cup her face in my hands, thumbs catching the wetness on her cheeks. "Let me be the one who stays."

She looks up at me, all that fear and hope warring in her eyes.

Then she whispers, "Okay."

The teddy bear hits the floor.

I kiss her slow and sure—no hesitation, no holding back. Just her and me and two weeks of dancing around this moment finally giving way to something that feels like coming home.

She melts into me, fingers curling into my shirt, and when she sighs against my mouth it undoes me completely.

When we finally break apart, she stays close, forehead against mine, breathing hard.

"So," I murmur, tucking a strand of hair behind her ear, "does this mean you're officially my girlfriend now?"

She laughs—soft and watery and perfect. "I guess it does."

"Say it." I brush my thumb across her cheek. "I want to hear you say it."

Her face flushes pink. "You're impossible."

"Say it, Gabby."

She rolls her eyes, but she's smiling. "Fine. I'm your girlfriend."

"Yeah, you are." I grin, pulling her closer. "And just so we're clear—I'm never letting you go."

"That's a little intense for eight in the morning."

"Get used to it." I kiss her forehead, then the tip of her nose. "Because I have plans for us. Real dates where I pick you up at the door. More dances—and not just the ones you owe me. Probably way too many terrible Valentine's puns."

"I'm already regretting this."

"Liar." I tilt her chin up, forcing her to meet my eyes. "You're not regretting a single thing."

Her breath catches. "No," she admits softly. "I'm really not."

I slide my hand to the small of her back, fitting her against me until there's no space left between us. She melts into my chest like she was made for this exact spot, her fingers playing with the fabric of my shirt.

Through the window, morning light spills across us, turning everything golden—the roses, the scattered petals, her hair catching fire in the sun.

"Hey Gabby?" I say into the quiet, my voice low against her ear.

"Yeah?"

"I'm really glad you showed up today."

She tilts her head back to look at me, eyes still shining, that smile I love breaking across her face. "Me too."

I brush my lips against her temple. "Thought you were skipping Valentine's Day."

Her smile widens—genuine and unguarded and so beautiful it stops my heart. She reaches up, fingers tracing the line of my jaw. "Turns out," she says softly, "I didn't want to skip it after all."

"Good." I catch her hand, pressing a kiss to her palm. "Because I wasn't going to let you."

And in the morning light of my chaotic apartment, with Valentine's decorations everywhere and a teddy bear as our only witness, Gabby Wallace finally stops running.

She came back to Ashen Mills to skip Valentine's Day.

Turns out, she just needed the right reason to celebrate it.

acknowledgments

So...this book has been my little secret for quite some time. When I got the wild idea to write a Valentine's Day novella, I knew one thing for sure: I didn't want to do it alone.

Good thing social media exists, right? Because that's where I found some incredible authors who were crazy enough to say yes to collaborating with me.

Jordan Riley, Cheyenne Pajardo, and Melissa Huffman—y'all are absolute rockstars. Thank you for putting up with my aggressively colorful spread-sheets, my radio silence followed by message explosions, and somehow still being my friends after all of it. You're the best!

Huge thank you to Jesus for showing me what true love really is and for helping me weave that into every page of this story. None of this happens without Him.

To my husband—once again, you kept our lives from falling apart while I locked myself away in both a fictional town and my office. You're my real-life romance hero, and I don't say that enough.

And to YOU, my amazing readers—whether you're holding a paperback or ebook, thank you for being here. Your support is the greatest love story of all.

Hi, I'm Amber and I write Christian romance!

You know those swoony moments that make your heart do a little flip? The second chances that remind us grace is real? That's what I love to write about—stories filled with hope, heart, and a whole lot of Jesus.

I used to write steamy romance, but God had other plans. He stirred my heart to shift directions, trading heat for heart and telling stories that honor my faith. Spoiler alert: best decision ever!

I also write clean, kisses-only romance under the pen name Erin Renee, because apparently one pen name wasn't enough chaos for my life.

When I'm not writing, you can find me being a wife to my high school sweetheart, wrangling three kids, and always—*always*—reading. Like, dangerously close to missing bedtime because "just one more chapter" turned into five.

I'm powered by Jesus, Alani energy drinks, and an unhealthy obsession with Nerds Clusters. Don't ask me to choose between the candy or the drinks. I can't.

Follow me on social media for all the bookish updates and behind-the-scenes fun.

And if you've enjoyed one of my books, a review on Amazon or Goodreads would make this author's heart so happy!

authorambernicole.com

instagram.com/authorambernicole

facebook.com/authorambernicole

tiktok.com/@authorambernicole

goodreads.com/authorambernicole